The Chronicles of Ashford Landing
volume one: Worthy

by W. R. Finch

© 2025 W. R. Finch (2nd edition)

For my mom: sorry it took so long.

Chapter One — Loaf of Bread and Black Cats

Rowan knew the bakery's schedule better than its owner did. The dough went in at four. The first batch hit the shelves at six-thirty. The trash went out at seven-fifteen, exactly. It wasn't glamorous, but it was warm. Sort of.

The smell of bread clung to the alley like it was trying to help. It wasn't. His fingers were already numb, and the cold made every motion feel like gripping things through a glove full of needles. Still, he worked quickly, lifting the lid of the green dumpster and bracing it with his shoulder as he leaned in.

No meat. No dairy. Nothing too soft. Mold was the real enemy. But every now and then, a loaf would be tossed for being too brown, or a bagel would break and get thrown out whole. Today, he hit gold.

A still-sealed bag of mini croissants. Slightly smushed, but otherwise untouched. Breakfast.

He was about to slide down from the edge when he noticed her.

A woman. Across the street, under the pharmacy awning. One hand holding her coat shut, the other wrapped around a tall coffee cup. She wasn't staring, exactly, but she was watching. Her expression was hard to read. She didn't look like a local. Her coat was too tailored—long and charcoal gray, buttoned close at the waist like it belonged to someone who never rushed. Her boots were tall and heeled, suede, the kind that didn't see slush or salt. She stood like she wasn't cold. Like the wind hadn't touched her. Her hair was shoulder-length and fine, the color of wheat just before harvest, catching light in a way that made it shimmer gold, not yellow. A few strands had slipped loose in the wind and drifted along her cheek. Her skin was pale, but not fragile—like marble, smooth and still.

There was something ageless about her, like she could walk through a century unchanged. Not pretty in the way people aimed for, but beautiful in the way statues were—quiet, composed, impossible to ignore. Her face was angular but not severe, all long lines and soft shadows, like something carved rather than born. Her eyes were dark brown, but not soft. Deep, like polished obsidian. You didn't look into them. You were pulled.

Rowan was used to looks like that. Twelve, with dark hair that always seemed a little too long and eyes the color of a thunderstorm. His clothes were hand-me-downs in the worst sense—baggy where they shouldn't be, too tight where they mattered, stained in places even he didn't want to guess at. He didn't look like trouble. But he didn't look like safety either.

Rowan stared back just long enough to make sure she knew it didn't bother him. Then he dropped down, tucked the croissants into his pack, and started walking out of the alley.

She crossed the street to meet him.

He didn't look at her. Didn't break his stride.

When she caught up, she spoke.

"Wait."

He stopped, but he didn't turn around.

"I'm Selene," she said, her voice clear and steady. "I thought you might be hungry." She held out a small white paper bag. "It's just bread. Still warm. No strings."

Rowan didn't move. He didn't reach for the bag.

"I'm not a charity," he said, his voice colder than he meant. "Don't offer me pity."

Her gaze didn't shift. She was calm, composed, unwavering. "You looked cold," she added, like that was the only explanation needed.

He looked up, and for a split second, the light shifted in a way that made the air around him shimmer. A flash of blue flickered—so brief it was almost imperceptible—but Selene noticed it.

Her eyes narrowed just the slightest bit, her expression unreadable. But she didn't mention it. She didn't break her composure. "I'm still offering," she said.

Rowan turned and started to walk away.

The library was open, at least. It always opened early on Saturdays, and if he got there before the rush, he could claim the green chair by the radiator. Warmest seat in the place.

He liked the library. Not just for the books, though he read them. It was the silence. The structure. No one bothered you there.

He found a travel mug abandoned on one of the tables and took a cautious sip. Cold. Black. But it helped.

Then he spotted the muffin.

It sat on a napkin near the window, barely touched. Maybe someone got full. Maybe someone forgot. Either way, it was his now. He picked it up and wandered toward the back.

It wasn't stealing. Not really.

He slid into a booth-style nook between the stacks and pulled out the book he'd hidden the day before—a battered paperback on Norse mythology. He wasn't sure why he liked it. The gods were petty and dramatic. But the world-building was solid, and the idea of layered realms stuck with him.

He was halfway through a chapter on Yggdrasil when he noticed her.

Cardigan, glasses, tote bag, sharp eyes. She was watching him from the next row over, holding a book of her own.

"You're in my seat," she said.

Rowan raised an eyebrow. "Pretty sure this seat was abandoned by the gods."

She smirked. "They were never known for sharing."

He turned back to his book.

A pause. Then: "You're not from around here."

He didn't answer.

"You're not a library regular either, or you'd know I claim that chair every Saturday."

He sighed. "Well. Guess I'm the new god of chairs."

That made her laugh. Quiet, amused. "You're quick."

"I read."

"Then you'll need fuel." She nodded toward the muffin. "That looked like a bold choice."

He didn't respond.

"I'm Elysse."

The girl in the cardigan wasn't actually a girl. Rowan guessed early twenties, though something in her gaze felt older—like she'd done her growing up sideways, not linearly. She wore round brass glasses, an oversized olive sweater, jeans with worn-out knees, and scuffed boots that looked like they'd walked through stories instead of streets. Nothing about her looked fragile, but she didn't seem armored either. Just... present. Her hair was a soft russet brown, pulled into a loose braid that kept slipping over her shoulder. Her skin was pale with a dusting of freckles across the bridge of her nose, and her face had that kind of stillness people usually trained into themselves—like she was always a few steps ahead in the conversation, just waiting for everyone else to catch up. She didn't glow. But something about her edged sideways out of normal, like the world had made space for her without telling him why.

4

She didn't glow, exactly, but there was something gently out-of-step about her, like she moved half a second ahead of the world and turned back to wait for it to catch up.

Rowan didn't offer a name.

"Want me to buy you a coffee?"

"No."

"Tea?"

"No."

"Okay." She sat anyway on the floor beside the bookshelf, flipping open her novel. "Suit yourself."

They sat like that for a while—Rowan reading, Elysse occasionally glancing at him, as if trying to solve a puzzle. Eventually, he stood, tucked the book into his coat, and left without a word.

The sun was lower now. The streets were busier. Tourists dragged children in puffy coats and clutched mugs of overpriced cider. Rowan moved through them like smoke, slipping between groups and ducking past the corner market.

He didn't like being out this late, but it was the weekend. Less chance of patrols. More noise to disappear into. He made it to the storm drain just before the streetlights flickered on.

The ladder was slick, but he knew the way. Three steps down, pivot left, metal grating—gone. He'd pulled it loose weeks ago. Then the crawl. Then the drop. Then the quiet.

His hideout was little more than a carved-out nook in the old overflow tunnel—dry now, mostly. A few blankets. A candle stub. A pencil and a sketchpad he'd traded for weeks ago. He didn't draw often, but sometimes he liked to sketch faces he'd seen.

There was a woman on one page who looked suspiciously like Selene. Rowan wondered briefly how many times he'd seen her around town or rather... how many times she'd seen him.

He was about to light the candle when he heard a soft thud from above and froze.

There was a scritch; quiet and persistent.

He turned and saw it—a cat. Black as pitch, with emerald green eyes that shone like glass.

It didn't meow. Didn't move. Just sat on the ledge, judging him.

"Shoo," he said.

It blinked slowly but didn't flinch.

He lit the candle. The cat blinked. Once. Slowly.

Then it curled up like it'd been invited.

5

Rowan stared at it for a long moment before muttering, "Whatever," and crawling into his blankets.

Chapter Two — Unpredictable

Rowan woke up the way he always did—cold, stiff, and already on alert.

The blankets barely helped. The storm drain kept the wind off, but not the damp. His joints ached from sleeping on concrete, and a sharp pain lanced through his ribs from curling too tight in the night. He stretched cautiously, muscles sore and lungs catching on the bite of the morning air.

His stomach growled. He ignored it.

It was early, just before the town started moving. The best time—when the streets were still quiet, when he could blend in with the workers setting up for the day, locals too groggy to look too closely. He climbed out of the tunnel, wiped the grime off his hands, and slipped into the flow of the waking town. He kept his head down, hood pulled low, but it didn't hide much. His dark hair stuck out in messy strands, and his blue eyes—sharp, alert, too old for twelve—darted from window to alley as he walked.

He didn't go near the bakery. Not after yesterday.

Didn't go near the library either.

People remembered things. Not always on purpose, but enough. Enough to get him noticed. And Rowan didn't get noticed. That was the rule.

He kept his hood up, kept moving, eyes scanning the sidewalks, alleys, storefront windows. Watching for badges. Watching for anyone watching him.

He'd done this before. In a dozen other towns, across who knew how many states. You didn't survive three winters on the street by being predictable. And he never stayed predictable for long.

But Ashford Landing was smaller than he liked. Too many shopkeepers who knew each other. Too many regulars who would remember the kid in the threadbare coat. He needed to leave soon. Maybe tonight. Maybe tomorrow.

He ducked into a narrow side street and walked the length of it without looking back.

Then, he got careless.

There was a little market on the corner—a mix of groceries and seasonal junk stacked on crates. He didn't take much. Just a bruised apple off a bin near the edge. No one saw.

7

Or so he thought.

"Hey!" a voice called out behind him.

Rowan turned his head just enough to see. A woman—older, wrapped in a knit shawl—was waving down a police officer across the street.

She didn't sound angry. She wasn't yelling. Just... concerned.

That was worse.

Rowan didn't wait.

He ran.

The officer saw him bolt and shouted, "Hey! Kid!"

More voices joined in. Footsteps. Radios.

Rowan's breath hitched, and he pushed harder.

The back streets of Ashford Landing were a maze of brick walls, rusted fences, and alleys that turned without warning. He weaved through them like smoke, heart pounding, lungs burning.

His shoes barely held together, soles flapping as he cleared a broken fence and dropped into a side lot.

But they were closing in.

He heard it—the clipped echo of boots on pavement. A voice barking into a walkie. Another turning the corner behind him.

He had seconds.

That's when he saw it.

A storm drain, half-covered by rotted boards and last fall's leaves. Narrow. Sharp-edged. Just wide enough.

The echo of boots on pavement grew louder, too fast now. Rowan's heart thudded harder, the sound of his own feet pounding in his ears. No. They were closing in.

Rowan didn't hesitate.

He dropped to the ground and crawled fast, shoulder first, pushing through the narrow opening. The boards scraped his back and snagged his coat, but he forced himself through, teeth clenched.

Something sharp caught his arm.

He hissed, low and involuntary, as metal tore through his sleeve and caught skin beneath. But there was no time to stop, no time to check. He pulled himself into the dark and curled behind the stone ledge just inside the drain.

Boots pounded past above him.

Voices echoed, then faded.

He didn't move.

Didn't breathe.

His heart felt like it might crack his ribs.

Eventually, the silence came back. That long, humming quiet that filled the world after danger passed. Still, he waited. Longer than necessary. He always did.

When he was sure they were gone, he shifted. His coat was torn at the forearm, a streak of blood soaking into the lining. He pulled the fabric away and winced. Not deep. Just enough to sting like hell.

He wrapped it in the cleanest corner of his sleeve and crawled out.

The air outside had changed. Brighter. Colder. Sharper. The light had moved—late morning now, maybe edging toward noon. He was drenched, filthy, and bleeding. His legs felt like jelly from the sprint, and his ribs ached with every breath.

He cut through back alleys, staying low and out of sight. There was a tightness in his chest now—not from fear, but from the creeping realization that he didn't have much left. Not energy. Not options. Not time.

He passed a trash bin and stopped short.

Cinnamon.

It wasn't strong. Just a trace. But it cut through the cold like a memory—sweet, warm, wrapped in sugar and something earthy. He didn't know if it was bread , soap, potpourri, or something else entirely, but it made his stomach twist with hunger. He followed it without thinking, drawn by instinct more than reason.

That's when he realized where he was.

The alley opened into a loading area behind a narrow brick building. A faded wooden sign over the back door read Aubrey Apothecary, the paint peeling but still elegant. A set of recycling bins lined one wall, and a single trash can sat cracked open near the door.

He hesitated, caught between caution and need. Then he reached out and gently lifted the lid.

Before he could peer inside, the door creaked open.

Rowan spun back, ready to bolt.

But it wasn't a cop.

It was her.

Selene stepped out of the apothecary like she'd been expecting him—not surprised, not alarmed. Just there. Her coat hung neatly from her shoulders, sleeves rolled once at the cuffs. Wheat-colored hair was pulled into a simple knot, a few loose strands falling around her face. Her eyes met his, steady as ever.

She didn't look at the trash can. Didn't look at the blood on his coat.

She just said, "If you want work, I have some."

Rowan stared at her.

No pity. No pressure. No conditions.

Just a quiet offer.

He didn't answer right away. His guard was still up. But something in his shoulders eased.

His body tensed, instinctively preparing to refuse, but a part of him, the part that was exhausted and raw, felt an unexpected flicker of relief. He nodded, almost imperceptibly, before turning to leave, as if by leaving, he could hold onto the illusion of control.

Chapter Three — Something Like Normal

Rowan wasn't sure what made him come back.

Maybe it was the cold. Maybe it was the ache in his ribs. Maybe it was the cinnamon. Maybe it was the way Selene hadn't asked questions—just offered.

Whatever the reason, the next morning he found himself standing outside the apothecary's front door, staring at the glass like it might shatter if he touched it.

He wasn't even sure if the job was real. Maybe she'd just been polite. Maybe she'd changed her mind. Maybe it was a trap.

But then the door opened.

Rowan felt the weight of Selene's calm gaze as he stepped over the threshold. His fingers tingled, unsure if it was the cold or the weight of an unspoken promise. It was strange—being in a place that was warm and kind without a catch. No strings, she had said. He wondered how long that could last.

Selene stood there, coat already off, sleeves rolled to her elbows like she'd been working for hours. She didn't look surprised.

"You're late," she said calmly, stepping aside.

"I didn't say I was coming."

"You didn't have to."

Rowan hesitated, the first thing he noticed was the smell.

Warm and strange. A mix of dried herbs, old wood, and something vaguely citrusy—clean, but not sharp. The place felt lived-in. Every surface was packed but organized there was a green velvet chair in the far corner that looked like it had absorbed a hundred years of stories. The floorboards creaked with intention—like they remembered every footstep that had come through. The air had that comforting weight of old wood and plant oil, with just enough dust to feel honest. A faded photograph of the building, back when it had a horse post instead of a sidewalk, hung near the door, slightly crooked. : jars labeled in handwritten script, bundles of dried plants hanging from hooks, copper tins stacked like alchemy kits. There was no music, no ticking clock, just the rustle of paper and the quiet creak of old floors.

The counter was polished wood, the back wall lined with tiny drawers and cabinets, like an apothecary from another century that had kept evolving.

He didn't know what he expected, but it wasn't this.

Selene moved behind the counter and pulled out a small clipboard. "You'll start with shelving and sweeping. Nothing complicated."

Rowan nodded slowly.

"I have clothes for you," she added. "They might be a little big, but they're clean. Bathroom's through there."

She gestured to a door behind the counter.

He hesitated.

She didn't push.

When he stepped through, he found a small but bright bathroom—clean tile, soft towels, a mirror that didn't make him look like a ghost. A stack of folded clothes sat on the edge of the sink: a soft black shirt, worn jeans, thick socks, and a pair of boots that looked barely used.

There was even a hair tie on top.

He stared at it for a long time.

When he came out, he looked almost like a different person. His hair was pulled back into a messy bun, still damp. The clothes were loose but warm. His coat was tucked under one arm, out of habit more than need.

Selene didn't comment. Just nodded and passed him a broom.

He took it silently.

Then a voice rang out from the back.

"Oh my gods, is that him?!"

Rowan flinched.

A woman barreled into the front room like a gust of chaos. Her red hair was coiled in a knot that might have started intentional and then given up halfway through. Bangs stuck to her forehead with sweat, and her sleeves were rolled to the elbow, arms dusted in something grayish and faintly glittery—possibly ash, possibly magic gone sideways. Her eyes were wide and green, but warmer than Selene's—more wildfire than forest. She moved like her body was half a sentence ahead of her brain. She looked like she lived in exclamation points.

"Please tell me this is him," she said, grinning. "You said he might come today, and look! He came!"

"Talia," Selene said dryly, "you're scaring him."

12

"I am scaring him," Talia agreed. Then to Rowan: "Hi. I'm Talia. You look like a wet rat and I mean that in the nicest possible way."
Rowan blinked. "Thanks?"
"That's a compliment here," she said solemnly.
He wasn't sure what to do with that.
"Come here," she added, grabbing a towel. "Your hair's a mess. Sit."
Selene didn't intervene. Rowan glanced between them, unsure, then sat on the stool she pulled out.

Talia got to work like a woman on a mission. She tugged his hair back, drying what was left of the damp, then tied it up neatly. Her hands were warm and surprisingly gentle, despite the nonstop commentary.
"I'm just saying, if you're going to work here, you've gotta look like you weren't raised by wolves, or at least the polite and civilized kind."
"That's oddly specific," Rowan muttered.
Talia grinned. "You're gonna do fine."
Just then, the front bell jingled.
A familiar voice floated in. "I brought cinnamon sticks, and if anyone tries to make me label another drawer, I'm disappearing into the void."
Elysse.
She stopped in the doorway, taking in the scene—Rowan in clean clothes, hair up, Talia mid-rant, Selene unbothered behind the counter.
She blinked once then smiled. "Looks like I missed something."

She slipped out of her coat like it was muscle memory, her cardigan patterned with stitched moths and moons Rowan hadn't noticed the first time. Her eyes crinkled at the corners when she smiled, but it didn't make her look younger—it just made her look like she knew things you didn't.
She set the cinnamon on the counter and raised an eyebrow at Rowan.
"So," she said. "Are you the new hire, or a very clean burglar?"
"He's the new hire," Selene said.
Rowan wasn't sure when that had been officially decided, but no one questioned it.
Talia plopped onto the counter beside the register, legs swinging.
"I already like him. He doesn't talk much, but he listens. That's rare."

"I'm not staying long," Rowan muttered.

"We're not keeping you," Elysse said. "You're choosing to be here. That's different."

He didn't know what to say, so he just shrugged.

Elysse extended a hand, palm up, like they were making a deal instead of an introduction. "Elysse. I handle the front sometimes, but mostly I'm here to keep the chaos under control."

"She's lying," Talia said. "She starts the chaos and then pretends it was mine."

"I observe the chaos and then write it down for the trial."

Rowan glanced between them, confused and vaguely alarmed.

"Ignore them," Selene said. "They get worse when they're fed."

For some reason that seemed to ease the tension in his shoulders.

Talia stuck out her hand dramatically. "You already know I'm Talia. I make things explode, smell nice, or sometimes both. You got a name, mystery boy?"

"Rowan."

"Rowan what?"

He paused, a beat too long and glanced around the room.

Talia caught it.

She didn't push, but something in her face flickered. She didn't press. Just nodded and said, "Cool. Rowan What. Got it."

Elysse shot her a look but said nothing.

A woman stepped out of the back hallway—tall, deliberate, wrapped in black like she hadn't dressed herself so much as let the shadows do it for her. Her long hair was ink-dark and braided with small silver pins that caught the light just enough to warn you not to underestimate her. Her face was sharper than Selene's, all symmetry and precision, and her skin was pale in that way that made her eyes even stranger. They were green—vivid, precise, almost backlit—and Rowan had the sudden, irrational thought that if you stared into them too long, you'd start telling her things you'd sworn to forget.

She looked directly at him.

Not a glance—a reading. Like she could see what he hadn't said yet.

She reached for a bundle of dried herbs near the door and said calmly:

"Try not to bleed on the rosehips. Talia gets dramatic about it."

Rowan blinked.

Before he could respond, she turned and walked out, vanishing into the back without a trace.

No one explained.

Talia didn't deny it.

Elysse just snorted. "She's not wrong."

Rowan kept staring at the doorway.

He didn't ask.

He wasn't sure he wanted to know.

Selene reached behind the counter and pulled something small from a drawer. A narrow notebook, plain but solid, with a soft leather cover and blank pages.

"Use it to track inventory. Or don't. Up to you."

Rowan took it carefully, like it might turn into something else if he moved too fast.

It was nothing special.

But it was his.

He nodded once. Almost invisible. Selene didn't react.

They didn't crowd him. Didn't act like they'd won. They just handed him a notebook and gave him space.

He stayed the rest of the afternoon.

Shelving. Sweeping. Watching the way people moved through the shop. Watching the way these strange women moved around each other—like orbiting stars that somehow never collided.

No one asked if he was okay.

No one asked where he'd been.

No one treated him like a problem.

And when Selene locked the door that night, she didn't say goodbye.

She just said, "See you tomorrow," like it was obvious.

Chapter Four — The Sesame Chicken Incident

Rowan swept the same section of floor three times before Selene took the broom from his hands and replaced it with a stack of empty jars.

"Restock," she said simply. "You're already good at acting invisible."

He didn't argue.

It had been two days since he started showing up in the mornings. The routine was the same: show up, do some menial tasks, listen to Talia and Lyra bicker while Elysse ran the books and Selene did an alarming number of tasks. He hadn't asked for anything. He kept his head down, did what was asked, and disappeared again when the day was done.

The shop changed around him in small ways. Mornings smelled like mint and citrus, afternoons like cedar and beeswax. The light shifted across the wide front windows as the day passed, catching on dust motes and the edge of copper tins. The creak of the floorboards had started to sound less like warning and more like rhythm.

But he hadn't eaten with them.

Not once.

Selene noticed first. She didn't say anything. Just watched.

Talia noticed next. And unlike Selene, Talia was loud.

"Okay," she said one afternoon, smacking the counter like she was buzzing in on a game show. "What do you eat?"

Rowan blinked. "What?"

"You heard me. We're ordering lunch, and you don't get to say 'I'm fine' again. That's not an answer. That's an evasion."

"I am fine."

"You're the kind of fine that faints in libraries," Talia said, already moving. "C'mon, work with me here. Food. Preferences. Go."

Rowan glanced between them—Talia half in her chair, Elysse cross-referencing takeout menus, Lyra sipping tea like this was a stakeout, and Selene watching it all with surgical calm.

"...Are you all related, or just aggressively coordinated?"

Talia grinned, wild and proud. "Mom runs the house, Aunt Lyra runs the chaos, and I run on spite, caffeine, and the occasional glitter explosion."

Her hair was pinned back with two mismatched barrettes that didn't actually hold anything. Her sleeves were uneven—one rolled to the elbow, the other still damp with something purple. Rowan had no idea what it was, and somehow, he already knew not to ask.

Elysse added without looking up, "She means Selene. She's our mother. And yes, it's as confusing as it sounds."

"I'm not hungry," Rowan muttered.

Selene, still labeling jars, said calmly, "It's part of your pay."

He turned toward her, confused. "What?"

"Lunch," she said. "You work, you eat. That's the deal."

Rowan glanced at Talia, who was now leaning over the counter with both elbows and an absolutely unhinged amount of focus.

"Alright," she said brightly, like this was the most important question of the century. "What's the last thing you ate that made you go 'Oh wow, I could eat this forever and die happy'?"

He shrugged. "I don't know. It was crunchy."

Talia gasped. "Crunchy how?"

Rowan hesitated. "Fried, I guess?"

"Was there sauce?"

"Yeah. I think so."

"What kind of sauce? Sweet? Spicy? Did it make your lips tingle or your brain go 'mm, yes, this is what joy tastes like'?"

Rowan blinked. "It was kind of sweet."

"YES. Was it red or brown? Come on, Rowan What, I'm building a profile here."

"I don't—brown?"

"Boneless or bones?"

"Boneless."

"Bite-sized?"

"Sort of?"

Talia clapped her hands like she'd just won bingo. "He means sesame chicken. He has to."

Selene, without looking up, added, "Extra rice. No peanuts."

"I'm ordering it right now," Talia said, whipping out her phone. "You better hope this is what you meant or I'm making you try five other kinds and ranking them on a flavor chart."

Elysse, fully entertained, offered, "We actually have a flavor chart."

"We do," Talia confirmed. "It's color-coded and everything."

Rowan just stared at them.

He wasn't used to being questioned like that—like it was a game, not a test.

And he definitely wasn't used to people trying this hard just to feed him.

When the delivery guy arrived, Rowan instinctively moved to the far end of the shop.

He didn't mean to. His body just did it.

Elysse took the bag with a practiced thank-you and zero small talk, while Talia vibrated behind her like a kid on Christmas morning.

The smell hit him first. Sweet, sharp, warm. Soy and honey and something gingery rose like steam through the room, blending with the usual herbal haze of the shop until it smelled like a potluck at a magical sleepover. It made Rowan's eyes sting before his stomach even caught up. It made something twist in his chest before his stomach even had a chance to growl.

"Okay!" Talia announced, setting the bag on the counter and flipping it open like she was presenting treasure. "Moment of truth, folks. Time to find out if Rowan has taste."

She pulled out the container, cracked it open, and shoved it toward him. "Here. Try. Now."

Rowan looked at it suspiciously. "What if it's not the same thing?"

"Then we try again tomorrow," Talia said, like it was obvious.

"That's not very efficient," he muttered.

"Neither is starvation," Elysse said without looking up.

He picked up a piece with the chopsticks—badly, like he'd only half seen how it worked once—and took a bite. The breading crunched softly, giving way to tender heat. Sweet sauce clung to the edges, sticky and familiar, and for just a second, it was like biting into a memory he hadn't earned. A real one. Not scrounged. Not stolen.

There was a long pause.

Then Rowan said, around the mouthful, "...This is the thing."

Talia exploded. "YES! I KNEW IT."

She did a spin, flung her arms in the air, and declared, "Ladies and future legend, I present to you: crispy, saucy, bite-sized vindication!"

"I'm writing that down," Elysse said, flipping open her notebook. "Crispy, saucy, bite-sized vindication.' Got it."

Rowan took another bite.

Then a third.

18

He didn't speak, but the tension in his shoulders started to melt. Just a little.

Talia slid a soda toward him and added, "That also comes with the meal. Don't argue. It's law."

He drank it without protest.

Selene watched from the far counter, her expression unreadable.

When Rowan finally stopped eating—half the container gone, but still guarded, like he might have to defend it from a dragon—Selene set down the jar she was labeling and said simply, "You can sleep here tonight. Back room. Couch. No one uses it."

Rowan blinked. "Why?"

"Because you're not much use to me if the cops grab you in the middle of the night," she said. "And they're getting too close."

He didn't ask how she knew.

He just nodded.

Selene handed him a folded blanket from behind the counter. "You can lock the door from the inside. Don't touch the blue cabinet. It bites."

Talia leaned in. "She's not kidding."

Elysse added, "It's locked for a reason."

Rowan didn't argue. He just took the blanket, nodded again, and disappeared into the back.

They didn't make a big deal out of it.

No speeches. No welcome. No trust-falls.

The back room smelled like cloves and old fabric. The couch springs creaked when he sat, but the blanket was thick and clean. He wrapped it tight around himself, letting the quiet settle into his bones.

Just a couch. A warm meal. And a door he could lock.

Chapter Five — Fever Dream

When Selene opened the shop that morning, she found Rowan still on the couch in the back room, curled under the blanket she'd given him.

At first, she thought he was asleep.

Then she stepped closer and saw the sweat on his forehead. The way his breath caught. His skin was pale, but flushed around the cheeks, and his whole body had that wrong kind of stillness—the kind that only comes with a fever.

His skin prickled like it couldn't decide if it was hot or cold. The blanket clung damply to him, the air pressing in like a second weight. His limbs ached—not the sharp kind of pain, but a slow, humming throb that made everything feel heavy.

"Rowan."

He didn't answer.

His eyes blinked open, glassy and slow, and then drifted shut again.

Selene's voice didn't change. "You're sick."

"I'm fine," he whispered.

"You're very bad at lying."

"I'm always cold in the mornings," he muttered.

"You're sweating."

He didn't argue.

There was a soft noise on the counter—paws landing. The cat perched beside a jar of dried hyssop, tail flicking like a metronome. She didn't blink. Just stared; Rowan stared back through bleary eyes, unsettled. He'd seen cats before—scrappy alley ones, twitchy house ones—but this one didn't move like a cat. She held herself like she was waiting for something.

Selene looked once, gave a faint nod, then turned back to him. "Can you walk?"

He managed to sit up, but that was about it. The motion made him sway, and he caught himself against the armrest, jaw clenched.

"I'll take that as a no."

"I can—"

"You don't have to."

Rowan didn't like that. Not the words. Not the tone. Not the fact that he couldn't stand up without feeling like the floor was going to tilt under him.

Selene turned toward the front.

"Elysse," she called, calm as ever.

The door opened immediately.

Talia followed.

"What's—oh," Talia said, the grin dropping from her face.

Selene nodded once toward the couch. "He's sick. I'm taking him to the house."

"Want me to come?"

"No."

She turned to Elysse. "You're in charge."

Elysse looked at Rowan, then back to Selene, and gave a single nod.

Talia started to protest, but Selene glanced at her. Just once.

Talia went quiet.

She knelt beside the couch, helped Rowan with his coat without asking, and pulled the blanket tighter around him. "Don't die," she muttered.

"I'm not dying."

"You look like you're dying."

He couldn't think of a comeback.

Selene held the door open.

Rowan stood slowly, legs shaky, balance worse. She didn't touch him. Just walked a half-step ahead as he followed, one foot in front of the other, careful and slow.

The cat hopped off the counter and fell in behind them.

No one said anything else.

They left the shop behind.

The walk to the house blurred.

Rowan kept his head down, boots dragging. The cold wind slapped his face, but it didn't help much. His thoughts were thick, slow. The edges of the world had gone soft. Selene didn't speak, didn't rush him. She just stayed close, matching his pace, guiding him through side streets and narrow turns until the town fell away behind them.

A long gravel drive stretched ahead, winding up through bare trees.

At the end of it stood the house.

Aubrey Manor.

It didn't look like the mansions Rowan had read about in books—no iron gates or perfect hedges. It was older, quieter. The kind of house that didn't care if you noticed it. Three stories tall, roof lines uneven from age and repairs. White oak beams framed weathered stone, and the windows had thick, imperfect glass that caught the light strangely.

It didn't look abandoned.

It looked patient.

Selene opened the door with a key that looked like it should belong to a church.

Rowan stepped inside and immediately felt the difference.

The air was warmer, but it wasn't just temperature—it felt layered, like the house had wrapped itself around him the second he crossed the threshold. The hardwood floors creaked softly under his boots. The walls were lined with portraits and shelves. No dust. No noise. Just a hush, deep and slow and old.

He stumbled.

Selene caught his arm—not tight, just enough.

"Upstairs," she said. "Guest room."

Rowan looked at the staircase and knew, absolutely, that he wasn't going to make it.

Selene glanced down the hall. "Lyra."

There was a soft pat of footsteps, and then the cat's eyes flicked toward him—green, sharp, reflective. In a flash, the cat shifted, the fur rippling and flowing as if it were a cloak being undone. The eyes—those same green eyes—locked onto his, but now the shape was human, tall, composed, and just as unreadable. Rowan didn't recoil. He just stared, too far gone to register fear. Some part of him filed it away as a dream. A strange, aching dream with claws.

Her hair was braided now, tied back in a way that made her look even sharper. She didn't say anything, just crossed the space between them and looped Rowan's other arm over her shoulder like she'd done it a hundred times.

She was stronger than she looked.

They got him up the stairs, slow but steady, Rowan half-conscious by the time they reached the landing.

The guest room door opened without a sound.

White sheets. Heavy quilts. The smell of eucalyptus and something older—something bitter and familiar. Selene and Lyra eased him down onto the bed. He tried to sit up, but Selene pressed two fingers to his chest, gentle but immovable.

"Don't," she said.

Lyra didn't leave yet.

Selene unbuttoned his coat, then his shirt, eyes narrowing as she reached his arm. There it was: a long cut tracing down his forearm.

Red, swollen, and clearly infected. Angry skin bloomed around the wound, heat radiating off of it like a coal under the surface. It pulsed in time with his heartbeat, a dull throb beneath the heat. The skin around it looked stretched too tight, the kind of wound that pulled the rest of the body into its orbit. He couldn't remember when it started to hurt—only that it had become part of him now, a slow-burning fuse he hadn't wanted to admit existed. Behind her, Lyra tilted her head slightly.

"Well," she said, voice dry as parchment, "I'd say that explains the dramatic fainting."

Rowan groaned softly.

"He's not dying," Selene muttered.

"Not yet," Lyra replied. "Give him two more days of pride and poor judgment."

Selene shot her a look. Lyra didn't flinch.

She disappeared into the hall without another word, soft-footed and silent.

Rowan barely registered any of it, already sliding deeper into the haze.

Selene didn't curse. Didn't panic. She just moved.

A basin appeared. Clean cloth. A little glass jar of something pungent and green. Rowan flinched when she touched it to the wound, and again when she wrapped it in something cool.

"You should've said something," she murmured.

"Didn't want to be a problem," he slurred.

"You already are. That's not the same as being unwanted."

He tried to make sense of that, but the fever pulled too hard.

He sank into the pillows and let the dark take him. The last thing he felt was the weight of the blanket being pulled higher. Not tucked. Not swaddled. Just placed—like a shield. A promise, maybe. That someone would still be there when the dark let go.

Chapter Six — Side Effects

Rowan woke in pieces.

First, it was the sound of birds—too many of them, too loud, like someone had turned the volume up on the outside world.

Then it was the light bleeding through old curtains, soft and gold and far too bright.

Then the weight of the blankets.

It was like the air itself was too thick, pressing down on his chest, a dull throb behind his eyes that didn't fade with each blink. His body felt heavier than it should. He blinked at the ceiling, unmoving.

Everything was still.

The bed was too soft.

The air was too clean.

The sheets smelled faintly of cedar and something faintly floral—not the cheap kind from laundromats, but something old-fashioned and handmade. A crocheted quilt lay across the foot of the bed, heavy with the weight of real thread and time. The room had one window, the glass imperfect, making the morning light shimmer like a dream.

It didn't feel like the shop. It didn't feel like anywhere he'd ever been.

He sat up, slowly, every movement dragging like someone had replaced his bones with sandbags. His arm throbbed immediately—low and hot. The bandage was clean and tight, his shirt replaced with something soft and too big.

For a split second, he panicked.

Where were his things?

He swung his legs over the side of the bed, dizzy but pushing through it. His boots were on the rug beside the nightstand. His coat, folded. His notebook—untouched, closed, placed on top of the stack like a bookmark he hadn't earned.

He let out a breath he hadn't realized he was holding.

The door creaked open before he could stand.

"You'll fall over," Lyra said, stepping into the room with a tray in her hands.

She wore her usual black wool dress—her silhouette looked like it had been drawn in ink—sharp, deliberate, with no room for smudges. The kind of presence that made silence feel intentional. Her posture was straight, but not rigid. Like she'd been trained to fight and taught not to bother unless it was worth her time. The tray held a steaming bowl, a chipped mug, and two folded napkins, one of which was currently being used as a coaster for something herbal and probably disgusting.

"I'm fine," Rowan said.

"You're dehydrated, half-starved, and still running a fever."

"That's better than yesterday."

"Not a high bar."

She set the tray on the dresser instead of handing it to him. Didn't come closer. Just folded her arms and leaned against the wall, watching him like he was a half-wild animal that might bolt if cornered.

"You slept twenty-one hours," she said.

"That seems excessive."

"Tell that to your immune system."

He rubbed his face with one hand, trying to ground himself. "I should go."

"Where?"

That shut him up. He didn't have an answer. Not one that wouldn't sound pathetic or paranoid or like a lie told too often. The idea of "where" didn't make sense anymore. It wasn't a direction—it was a defense.

Lyra didn't press. She just stood there, quiet, waiting.

"I didn't mean to stay this long," he said eventually.

"You also didn't mean to get infected, pass out, or wake up in my house," she replied. "And yet, here we are."

Rowan didn't touch the tray, but he didn't tell her to take it away, either.

Lyra stayed against the wall, arms still folded, like she wasn't going anywhere until he gave in.

A few minutes passed in silence before footsteps echoed up the stairs.

The door swung open and Talia burst in, carrying a second blanket and absolutely no restraint. Her jacket was half-zipped, mismatched socks visible under her boots, and her braid was lopsided like she'd run out the door halfway through tying it. She moved like a storm on the verge of mischief.

"He's alive!" she announced. "Someone tell the underworld they can't have him yet."

"Can we not shout?" Rowan said, eyes half-shut.

"Okay, but you didn't deny it," Talia muttered, setting the blanket at the foot of the bed. "I knew it. You're secretly the dramatic one."

Elysse followed, holding a small jar of something pale and glowing. "I made you tea," she said. "Which is a lie. Selene made it. But I watched, which counts."

Rowan blinked at the jar. "That's not tea."

"It's medicinal."

"So it tastes bad."

"Correct."

Lyra finally stepped away from the wall and opened the window halfway. Crisp air spilled in, chasing out the dense warmth of fever-sick skin and herbal steam.

Rowan sat quietly, trying not to fall sideways.

"Do you want anything?" Elysse asked, surprisingly gentle.

"No."

"Too bad," Talia said. "We brought half the pantry just in case. There's a croissant downstairs with your name on it. I'm lying. We ate it. But we can lie again."

"I don't want—"

"We know," Lyra said. "You don't want anything. You're not staying. You're not attached. You're just here until you can walk again, and then you'll vanish."

Rowan looked at her.

She didn't flinch.

"Cool," Talia muttered. "Way to go for the jugular."

"He knows," Lyra said. "I'm just saving him the speech."

Rowan didn't answer.

He leaned back into the pillows, too tired to argue. Too sick to storm off. Too aware that if he moved wrong, he'd vomit or collapse or both.

They didn't say it out loud, but something shifted then.

The room didn't feel like a guest room anymore.

It felt like a waiting place. A space quietly being held open, in case he decided to claim it.

The room had gone quiet again, tension cooling like steam off a kettle.

Talia, apparently allergic to silence, plopped onto the foot of the bed and said, "Okay. Since you're not dying, I can tell you about the woman who came in today and tried to return dried sage because it wasn't 'aesthetically smudgy enough.'"

26

"She wanted it curlier," Elysse added, deadpan.

"She wanted it to look like the ocean breeze had personally styled it," Talia said. "I said it's sage, not seafoam mousse."

Rowan blinked at them. "...That didn't happen."

Talia gasped, scandalized. "How dare you. That woman was real. She brought mood boards."

"She printed them," Elysse confirmed.

Rowan didn't mean to smile. But he did.

And while he was distracted, Talia nudged the tray on the dresser a little closer. "You know, most people would be grateful to eat luxury sage. This could've been you."

"I don't even like sage."

"You've never had our sage."

Rowan, halfway through a retort, took a bite of the soup.

He didn't seem to notice he'd done it.

"Then there was the guy who asked if we sold 'handmade mushrooms,'" Elysse said, pulling a book from her bag like she was about to cite sources. "When I asked if he meant dried or powdered, he said, 'no, the artisanal kind. Locally grown, but, you know—crafted.'"

"He wanted bespoke fungi," Talia said, shoving a pillow behind Rowan's back like she'd been planning it all along. "Like mushrooms with personality."

"I thought he was high," Elysse said. "Turns out, he just moved here from Vermont."

Selene appeared in the doorway with a second plate—something breaded, something warm.

She didn't say anything. Just set it on the tray, took the empty bowl, and vanished again like she'd never been there.

Rowan picked up the fork without thinking.

"Anyway," Talia continued, watching him out of the corner of her eye like a proud hunter, "I told mushroom guy we only carry emotionally balanced chanterelles."

"You didn't."

"I absolutely did. I said the morels had recently been through a breakup and weren't seeing customers."

Rowan shook his head, smiling again in spite of himself.

He finished the second plate.

He didn't notice that either.

Rowan leaned back against the pillows, the plate empty, his eyelids heavier by the second.

He yawned without warning—full-bodied, jaw-cracking, the kind that takes your soul with it.

Talia looked deeply offended. "Did you just yawn in the face of my storytelling?"

"He's exhausted," Elysse said, rising from the chair. "We've done our job."

"Fine," Talia muttered, standing. "But I'm coming back with jokes tomorrow."

Rowan blinked slowly. "Don't."

Talia grinned. "Too late."

Elysse gave him a nod on the way out—almost a salute, like a quiet you survived. Lyra was the last to move, pausing at the doorway just long enough to say, "Try not to relapse. I don't like repeating myself." Then she was gone.

      The room was quiet again. The faint scent of cedar lingered. Somewhere in the distance, a floorboard creaked like a sigh. Rowan stared at the ceiling, heart steady now, full in a way he didn't quite have words for.

Rowan didn't remember falling asleep.

But when he woke next, someone had tucked the blanket over him, and the tray was gone.

Chapter Seven — The Hook by the Door

Rowan woke up thinking he was somewhere else. That happened sometimes. When he'd stayed too long in one place, or slept somewhere safe, or eaten too well the night before. His brain kicked back into flight mode before his body caught up.

The ceiling was too high. The bed too soft. The silence too comfortable.

For one stretched-out moment, he couldn't remember where he was.

Then the smell of cinnamon drifted in from downstairs, and something in his chest clicked back into place.

He sat up slowly, the morning sun leaking in through tall windows—old glass, the kind with warping that made the outside world shimmer like a dream. The fever was gone. The ache in his joints had faded to a dull memory. His body felt less like a survival machine and more like something he lived in.

There was weight to him now. The kind of weight that only came from sleeping more than one night in the same bed. From not needing to wake up ready to run. Even the blankets began to feel like they belonged to him.

He looked over.

The closet on the far wall had been cracked open. Inside, hung neatly on wooden hangers, were clothes that weren't his—but were for him. Shirts, sweaters, jeans in his size. Folded extras on the shelf above, right down to socks and gloves.

Rowan stared at it.

Not long. Just long enough to register that it was real.

He stood, padded to the small mirror above the dresser, and ran a hand through his hair. He still looked tired, but not haunted. Not like he was falling apart.

In the bathroom, there was a toothbrush in a cup, a new one: still in the wrapper, but placed beside the others like it had always been there.

He brushed his teeth in knowing silence.

When he made his way downstairs, there was a coat hook near the front door—slightly lower than the rest. Just enough to be eye-level with him. He didn't remember seeing it there before.

The house creaked softly under his steps. Aubrey Manor was full of sounds like that—settling noises, like the whole place was breathing. The hallways were wide, lined with books and crooked picture frames. The furniture looked like it had lived here longer than anyone else. Some of it mismatched. Some of it old enough to whisper.

None of it was fancy, but all of it was cared for. Each item came with a history and some with a warning label.

He followed the smell of cinnamon toward the kitchen, sunlight cutting warm paths across the floorboards. Voices murmured low from the other room, casual and familiar. Someone was humming.

He found the breakfast table already set—half full mugs, a dish of eggs, toast, jam, something that looked suspiciously like Talia's attempt at baking.

He hesitated at the threshold, just for a second.

Then he sat down.

"Over easy is superior," Talia was saying as Rowan walked in. "It's the perfect texture-to-toast-ratio egg. You can dip in it."

"Scrambled doesn't run," Lyra replied flatly. "Some of us don't enjoy their breakfast bleeding."

"That's rich coming from someone who ate a mouse last week."

"He got into my crackers," Lyra said without missing a beat. "He had it coming."

Talia threw up her hands. "You can't eat someone over snacks!"

"I did."

"You're supposed to be civilized!"

"I'm not."

Rowan sat down at the table as they continued.

There was a plate already in front of him.

He stared at it.

Eggs, over easy. Two of them, perfectly cooked. Pancakes—stacked, buttered, no syrup. A cup of black coffee at his side, still steaming. No one had asked. No one had said a word. The fork was tucked under a napkin like it had been waiting for him specifically.

He looked around the table.

They were still arguing like it was a national emergency.

He blinked.

"Wait a second," he said slowly.

Talia paused, mid-sentence.

"You..." Rowan squinted at the plate. "You tricked me."

Elysse looked up from her book across the table. "It took you long enough."

Rowan pointed at the pancakes like they were evidence in a crime. "You watched me eat and figured out my order."

"Obviously," Lyra said.

Talia grinned. "We're incredibly dangerous."

"You tracked me like a predator."

"You say that like it's a bad thing."

"I do," Rowan muttered, but there was no heat behind it. Just the creeping certainty that they'd seen something in him he hadn't seen yet.

Selene walked in just then, topped off his coffee, and walked out again without a word.

Rowan stared at the door she'd just exited through.

"You're all insane."

"Possibly," Elysse said.

"But you ate the whole plate," Lyra noted, already sipping her tea.

Rowan grumbled something into his coffee and didn't look up again before pushing his plate back an inch and staring at it like it had betrayed him.

"You've been doing this the whole time," he said. "Tracking what I eat. What I like. The clothes, the toothbrush, the hook by the door —none of that just happened."

Talia opened her mouth.

"Don't say it's hospitality." Rowan snapped.

She closed it.

"I didn't agree to this," he said, softer now. "I didn't ask for a room. I didn't ask for a house. I didn't ask for—"

He cut himself off.

Lyra didn't blink. "You didn't have to."

He looked around the table. No one looked sorry. No one looked surprised.

Rowan pressed both hands flat against the wood, fingers trembling slightly. "You're all acting like I live here."

The silence that followed wasn't heavy.

It was simple.

Obvious.

Rowan buried his face in his hands trying to hold back the flood of emotion, without warning a light bulb overhead exploded causing glass to scatter in tiny sparks around him. He flinched and shut his eyes tightly as the room went silent.

A moment later opened his eyes slowly, chest heaving. The broken glass glittered like ice across the floor.
No one screamed. No one demanded to know what just happened.
Talia smirked. "There it is."

Chapter Eight — Spark

Rowan stared at the ceiling, his mind still whirring from what just happened.

Glass glittered on the table. No one had moved. No one had yelled. He braced for the inevitable.

"What was that?" he asked, voice low, almost to himself.

Talia leaned forward, her eyes narrowed in focus. "That was magic," she said, matter-of-fact, as if she were explaining a simple fact.

"It was an accident," Rowan muttered, his hands still trembling slightly from the surge of power. His fingertips tingled like they'd been scalded, nerves jittery from inside out. His ribs felt tight. Not pain exactly—just pressure, as if something had pushed outward from his chest and hadn't fully gone back in.

Elysse looked up, clearly taking notes. "You sparked without contact. That's rare. Most people need something to trigger it."

Rowan frowned, confusion still written all over his face. "I broke something."

Lyra, unmoved, crossed her arms. "You're a teenager. You break things."

Selene, entering with her usual quiet presence, placed a short black candle and a book of matches in front of him. "Try again," her voice didn't rise, didn't demand. But it held something firmer than authority—expectation. Like she already knew the outcome and wasn't worried about the mess in between.

Rowan blinked. "You want me to break another light bulb?"

"No," she said, her tone unchanged. "Light the candle."

Rowan shot a look at the others. They were watching him closely. Talia grinned, waiting expectantly.

Rowan couldn't help but scoff. "This is ridiculous. Magic isn't real."

There was a brief silence.

Then Talia tilted her head, her voice flat, as if she were addressing something obvious. "You just shattered a light bulb with your brain. While having an emotional breakdown over toast. Magic's real."

"That could've been static electricity," Rowan said, not convinced.

Elysse, without missing a beat, added, "Don't even joke about that in front of Selene."

Rowan shook his head, still trying to come up with a rational explanation. "Maybe it was wiring or—something. Coincidence."

Talia raised an eyebrow, unimpressed. "You're embarrassing our ancestors."

"I didn't ask to have ancestors!" Rowan shot back, though his words lacked conviction.

Lyra, leaning against the wall, sighed. "You're spiraling. It's cute."

Rowan opened his mouth to retort, but Talia, ever the interrupter, raised a hand and stood up. With a dramatic flick of her wrist, she held her hand over the candle.

Nothing happened.

Talia's brows furrowed. "Don't ruin this for me," she muttered, staring at the wick.

Then, in an instant, the flame leapt to life.

Talia dropped back into her seat, clearly pleased with herself. "There you go. Real enough for you?"

Rowan blinked at her. "You used a match."

"Nope," she said, still smiling. "Just a little flair."

Rowan glared at the candle, exasperated. "Fine. But I'm not doing that."He didn't like how fast everything moved. How fast *they* seemed to accept what he couldn't even name yet. Magic; the word tasted like fiction in his head. He'd stopped believing in that sort of thing a long time ago.

"Come on," Talia coaxed. "What's the worst that could happen?"

"I could break something again," Rowan muttered.

Elysse, glancing up from her book, responded casually, "The candle costs eighty cents."

Lyra, ever practical, added, "It's from a throwaway batch. Didn't pass the scent test."

Rowan blinked. "What was it supposed to smell like?"

"Rain and redemption," Talia said with a snort. "It ended up smelling like wet cardboard and lies."

Elysse; without looking up, "We use them when customers annoy us."

"That..." Rowan muttered, "That also doesn't make me feel better."

"Good," Lyra replied. "Now you're learning."

Selene stood by, watching quietly, letting him process. She made no move to rush him.

Rowan stared at the candle, still flickering innocently. He let out a frustrated breath. "Fine."

He focused, tried to feel something—anything.

There was a faint crackle in the air.

Rowan's eyes widened. The hair on his arms stood up. The air around his hands felt charged, humming like a wire too close to breaking. A coppery taste filled his mouth. Something stirred in his chest—like fear and memory knotted together.

"Uh," he said, feeling the static charge building.

Before anyone could respond, the candle exploded.

Not violently—just a sharp crack of electricity, the flame vanishing in a flash, and the base flipping off the table with a small puff of smoke.

Rowan recoiled. "I didn't—!"

"Yes!" Talia shouted, her fists raised. "That was amazing!"

"I destroyed it!" Rowan said, shocked.

"That's progress," Elysse said, already scribbling something down.

Lyra leaned over, snuffing out the smoke with a casual motion. "You're definitely one of us."

Rowan looked around the table, his heart still racing. No one was angry. In fact, they were all smiling.

He sat back down, the buzzing in his ears finally starting to calm down.

Selene, without comment, replaced the candle with a new one. Rowan looked at her, trying to read her expression. There was no surprise. No worry. Just the steady calm of someone who'd seen fire before—and knew exactly what to do with it.

Chapter Nine — Ember

The new candle sat on the table. Rowan glared at it.

He had been trying for hours. Between chores, between questions, between sarcastic commentary from Talia and increasingly detailed diagrams from Elysse, he'd come back to the same chair, same candle, same flickering failure.

He was close. He could feel it. His hands tingled sometimes. Once, the flame had wobbled like it was going to catch—but it hadn't. Now it was nearly dinnertime. His hands ached. His head buzzed. The candle didn't care.

Talia was upstairs, humming. Elysse had gone out to run an errand. Selene was in the kitchen, something warm and garlic-heavy drifting out with every pass of the spoon.

Lyra sat across the table, sipping her tea, watching him.

She hadn't said anything in almost twenty minutes.

Which meant, obviously, she was about to drop something he didn't want to hear.

"You're trying to light it like Talia," she said finally. "Stop."

Rowan looked up. "What?"

"You keep forcing it. Fire's not your thing. Not like that."

"I thought fire was the goal."

"It is. But you're not her. You don't do magic by flexing. You do it by listening."

Rowan stared at the candle. "Listening to what, exactly?"

Lyra shrugged. "Yourself."

He looked back down.

The candle sat there.

Small. Unimpressed. Waiting.

Rowan stared at the candle and tried not to think.

Not about Talia's flare.

Not about Elysse's diagrams.

Not about Lyra watching him like she was waiting for a punchline.

He just sat.

Breathed.

He let his fingers hover near the table—not too close, not reaching, just ready. The buzz in his skin was still there, low and quiet, like static waiting for a signal. Listening to it rather than trying to push.

A faint tingle built behind his fingertips, like something coiling inward instead of lashing out.

Rowan lifted one hand—two fingers raised—and let it go.

A single, sharp spark jumped from his fingertip to the wick.

The candle caught instantly.

A tiny flare, blue at the center, flickering to gold.

No explosion.

Just control.

Rowan stared at it, heart thudding. The flame held.

Lyra didn't clap. She just nodded once, like the universe had finally corrected itself.

Selene's voice floated in from the hallway. "Dinner."

Rowan sat back, the faint smell of ozone still clinging to the air.

"I did it," he said, half-laughing. "I lit it."

Talia looked up from the bowl she was stealing biscuits out of. "Wait—you did it?"

"Little spark. Right from my fingers."

"YES." She punched the air. "I knew you had it in you."

Selene was already setting out plates, unfazed. "Good. You'll be practicing again tomorrow."

Lyra raised her glass slightly, deadpan. "Congratulations on not frying the table."

Rowan sat down, a little breathless but grinning for real now, that strange warmth still in his chest.

Elysse passed the breadbasket across the table. "Now that you've proven you're not going to accidentally ignite the curtains, we can move on to the next phase."

"What's the next phase?" Rowan asked, still catching his breath.

"Academic placement."

He froze. "What?"

Elysse set down her fork, meeting his gaze. "Math, history, reading. Magic isn't all we're teaching here. If you're going to be here, you're going to need to catch up. A baseline, you know?"

"You're giving me a test?"

"I'm giving you a baseline," she said, cutting her food calmly. "And maybe a little trauma."

Rowan blinked. "You people are relentless."

"We're thorough," Selene corrected.

"You lit a candle," Talia said. "We threw a party. This is balance."

He looked around the table. Talia was licking butter off her fingers like she hadn't just stolen three biscuits. Elysse had already

annotated her napkin. Selene poured tea without asking who
wanted it. Lyra passed the salt with two fingers, like a silent dare.
Rowan's fork hovered over his plate. The food was hot. His chair
didn't creak.

Nobody was watching him.
A breeze from the open window stirred the candle's flame—his
candle.
It held.
He exhaled slowly and tucked one foot around the leg of the chair.
Just to anchor it.

Chapter Ten — Placement

The next morning, Rowan came downstairs to find Elysse waiting for him with a clipboard, a mug of coffee, and an expression that suggested mercy was off the table.

"Sit," she said, nodding toward the kitchen table.

"What did I do?"

"Nothing," she replied. "Yet."

Talia popped her head in from the pantry, arms full of something crunchy. "It's your academic assessment day!" she announced like it was a holiday. "We voted. You lost."

"I wasn't there to vote."

"Which means you lost by default," Lyra added, already halfway through her tea.

Rowan sat, eyeing the clipboard like it might sprout fangs.

Elysse placed it in front of him with precision. The top sheet read: Aubrey Household Academic Placement & Evaluation Form. In extremely elegant, suspiciously prepared handwriting.

"I made this myself," she said proudly.

He looked at her. Then the form. Then back at her.

"This seems... extremely prepared for someone who didn't expect me to stay."

There was a pause.

Talia turned around very slowly and said, "We're not saying it was a trap. But if it was a trap, it was very well designed."

Elysse cleared her throat and flipped the page. "Let's begin."

The first section was math.

It went badly.

Rowan stared at the problems like they were written in a forgotten language. He tried—he really did—but even the simple ones made his brain feel like it was short-circuiting.

After ten minutes of silence and suffering, he looked up and muttered, "I'm pretty sure numbers hate me."

"They don't," Elysse said. "They just don't know you yet."

"Then we should stay strangers."

Science was next.

Equally disastrous.

He blinked at a diagram of the water cycle and asked, in complete seriousness, "Is this a metaphor?"

By the time they reached history, his soul had all but left his body.

Until he saw the question: 'Name one historical figure you admire, and explain why.'

Rowan picked up the pen like it weighed nothing.

"Oh no," Talia whispered. "He's awake."

Rowan started writing.

Not slowly.

Not hesitantly.

Like the pen had been waiting all morning for something worth its ink.

He filled the entire answer section in about thirty seconds, flipped the page, and kept going.

Elysse blinked, stunned by how quickly Rowan had filled the page. "The question only asked for a paragraph." she opened her mouth to speak, voice quieter this time. "Tell me, who do you think... had the right idea?"

Rowan didn't look up. "He deserved more."

"Who?" Lyra asked.

"Caesar."

"Oh gods."

Rowan kept writing. "Everyone misses the point. They think the play's about betrayal, or ego, or leadership. It's not. It's a warning."

Elysse set her coffee down, eyes narrowing. "Go on."

"It's anti-war propaganda disguised as a tragedy," Rowan said, finally pausing. "Brutus thinks he's saving Rome, but he ends up accelerating its collapse. The conspirators kill Caesar, but they don't stop anything. They start everything. Bloodshed. Civil war. More death."

He looked up, eyes sparking—not magically this time, just with clarity.

"The message isn't 'Don't be Caesar,'" he said. "It's 'Don't be Brutus.' Don't kid yourself into thinking you can kill your way into peace. That's not how people work."

The room was quiet for a beat too long.

Even Talia, halfway through a mouthful of dried cereal, didn't move.

Then she whispered, "Damn."

Lyra sipped her tea. "How did you fail math and start a rebellion in the same hour?"

Elysse, still watching him, nodded once. "Alright. We'll skip the reading comprehension section."

Rowan blinked. "Wait, seriously?"

"You just rewrote my entire thesis from when I was eighteen."
Then she added, more quietly, "You still don't have the full context."
Rowan paused. "Then give it to me."
Elysse looked at him for a long moment. "Alright," she said. "But not all at once. We'll take it slow."
Talia added, "And you said 'civil war' without being weird about it. That's a win. You might just be her favorite student."

Rowan sat back in the chair, surprised at how winded he felt. His heart hadn't slowed yet; not from effort, but impact. For the first time he was being listened to: and it felt louder than yelling.

Elysse flipped through the pages, pausing here and there. She didn't smile, but she tapped the corner of the paper once with her nail—a habit she only did when something impressed her. .
Lyra gave him a nod that almost counted as praise. Talia had moved on to spinning an orange in place like it might unlock a secret.
But it was Selene who answered the question he hadn't asked yet. She stepped into the room, drying her hands on a towel, and said, "No one's waiting for you to leave."
Rowan blinked. "What?"
"You're allowed to be here," she said simply. "This isn't a deal. You don't have to earn it. You can rest."
He didn't say anything.
Because part of him had expected exactly that—that there was some unspoken condition. A test to pass. A door that would eventually close.

Rowan's hand hovered over the paper, not quite touching it —like permanence might smudge if he held it wrong. "I just..." He looked down at the paper. "This feels... permanent."

"It can be," Selene said. "If you want it. But you don't owe us anything. No contracts. No tests. Just a place."
She folded the towel, like it was just another task. "You're allowed."
That part mattered too.
She wasn't offering an out.
She was offering a choice.
And somehow, that felt even safer.
He didn't answer right away.
But he didn't leave the table, either.

Lyra took a long sip of her tea, then said dryly, "Great. Now we've emotionally adopted him. Do we all get matching jackets, or is this more of a secret handshake thing?"

Chapter Eleven — The Pattern

Rowan had a schedule now; which was weird.
Not bad—just weird.

Breakfast at eight. Magic practice at nine. Apothecary work until lunch. Then schoolwork in the afternoon, followed by another short burst of magic practice before dinner.
He didn't remember agreeing to it.
But somehow, it had just... formed around him.

No one barked orders. No one rang bells or made chore charts. Selene would just slide a plate in front of him at the same time every morning. Elysse would drop a math worksheet beside his toast. Talia would yell from across the shop floor, "Hey, candle-boy, you're on wick-trimming duty!" like it was the most natural thing in the world.
And it worked.

The magic drills were short—ten, maybe fifteen minutes. Just enough to tire him out a little without frying anything. They focused on precision. Control. Little things. Lighting candles. Sensing heat. Redirecting sparks instead of blasting them.

And when the surges came—those strange, sudden power spikes that made his hands buzz and the lights flicker—Selene didn't panic. She just nodded like she'd been expecting it.
Like she'd seen it before. He was still figuring out how he felt about that.
The apothecary had its own rhythm, older than all of them.
Built in the late 1800s, the place still creaked like it remembered boots and bustle skirts. The hardwood floors were worn smooth by a hundred years of footsteps, and the walls held the scent of lavender, citrus, and old magic that never quite aired out. Shelves ran the length of the main floor, crowded with jars and bottles—some labeled in tidy modern handwriting, others still bearing the faded scrawl of owners long gone. Bundles of herbs dangled upside down from ceiling beams darkened by time and steam.

A narrow staircase led up to a cramped loft where Talia liked to work and occasionally nap. The railing still bore her boot scuffs. In the back, a small kitchen had been converted into a workspace, half alchemy lab and half grandmother's pantry. The tile was cracked. The windows fogged easily. But it was clean. Always clean.

They stood side by side in the apothecary's back kitchen, squeezed between shelves of mason jars and mismatched copper pans. A wide farmhouse sink—porcelain, chipped at the edges—sat beneath the only window, which they'd cracked open to let the fumes out.

The walls were lined in old bead board, paint softened by heat and time. A faded paper charm was still pinned to the pantry door, yellow with age but humming faintly when Rowan passed. The air smelled sharp and herbal—rosemary, citrus, a whisper of lye, and something older buried beneath it all. Something almost familiar.

"Soap?" Rowan said, eyeing the materials on the counter like they might explode.

"Yes," Selene replied. "Soap."

"You're telling me I have literal lightning hands, and you want me to make bath supplies."

Selene measured lye into a ceramic bowl. "Lightning hands or not, you still stink after a full shift."

Rowan opened his mouth to argue, then shut it again. Fair point.

Selene handed him a pair of gloves and safety goggles.

"This feels unnecessarily dramatic," he muttered.

"Soap-making involves lye," she said. "Lye involves chemical burns. Drama is appropriate."

Rowan slid the goggles on. "This feels like a trap."

She handed him the bowl. "Pour slowly."

Despite himself, he leaned in.

There was something soothing about the process— measuring oils, heating them just enough, watching the mixture change as lye hit fat. It thickened slowly, the scent building into something rich and clean.

"Is this actually magic?" he asked.

"Sometimes," Selene said. "But mostly it's just knowing what works. Magic isn't always power. Sometimes it's precision."

Rowan stirred, eyes focused. "So this is, what—alchemy?"

"Tradition," she said. "And patience. The spellwork comes later."

By the time they poured the mixture into the mold, Rowan's shoulders had relaxed and the corners of his mouth had tugged upward.

Just a little.

"Alright," Selene said, wiping her hands on a cloth. "Go find Talia. She's expecting you."

44

"Should I be worried?"

"Yes," Selene said, without looking up.

Rowan stepped into the front room of the apothecary and immediately smelled chaos.

Specifically: cinnamon, lavender, wax, and what he could only describe as burnt ambition.

Talia was crouched on the floor, surrounded by glass jars, wax pitchers, silicone molds, and about four open bottles of essential oil—none of which were labeled correctly.

She looked up with wide eyes and a gleeful grin. "There he is. My apprentice. My protégé. My tiny wax goblin."

Rowan stared. "What happened here?"

"I got inspired."

"This smells like a headache and a fire hazard."

"Thank you."

She handed him a pitcher of melted wax and a pair of tongs. "You're going to pour while I figure out which of these bottles is eucalyptus and which one is definitely not eucalyptus."

"I feel like this is a test."

"It is," Talia said. "But it's also a trap."

Rowan stepped carefully between a few suspiciously glittery spills and tried to find a clear workspace. "Is there a reason there's glitter in the oven?"

"Memory loss spell went wrong," Talia muttered. "It's fine now. Mostly."

Rowan started pouring the wax, steady and slow, and weirdly... he liked it. The warmth. The process. The feeling of making something on purpose.

Talia sniffed one of the bottles, recoiled, and tossed it into the trash with no further comment.

"You're weirdly good at this," she said.

"I like order," he replied. "Even in chaos."

The bell above the door jingled.

Rowan barely looked up from labeling candles, but Lyra was already perched in the reading nook in the far corner, framed by high-backed chairs and a lace curtain someone had long since given up trying to keep white, hands folded neatly on the table like a fortune-telling cat.

A brass lamp with a cracked green shade bathed the table in soft light, catching the glint of Lyra's rings as she shuffled the cards. Beneath the table was a storage trunk, still marked with the initials of the apothecary's original owner—a midwife who, according to Talia, had once hexed the mayor for implying women shouldn't own property. The place had a memory for things like that.

The woman who entered was wearing designer everything —coat, heels, sunglasses tucked into her hair like a crown. Her perfume hit the room before she did.

She took her seat across from Lyra and leaned in, all hushed energy and lip-glossed desperation.

"I just want to know," she said, breathless. "Will I have a boyfriend by Christmas?"

Rowan paused mid-label.

Lyra didn't blink. She reached for her tarot deck and began to shuffle like she was weighing every bad life decision this woman had ever made.

She cut the deck. Drew three cards.

The Fool. The Tower. The Moon.

Rowan grimaced quietly from the candle station.

Lyra stared at the cards with the calm detachment of someone breaking difficult news to someone who absolutely deserved it.

She pointed to The Fool. "You keep stepping off cliffs."

The woman blinked. "Emotionally?"

"No," Lyra said. "Repeatedly. You ignore every red flag, label it a challenge, and then cry when it sets your car on fire."

Rowan dropped a candle label and clapped a hand over his mouth, trying not to choke on laughter.

It didn't work.

A single wheeze escaped. Talia gave him a high-five with her eyes.

Lyra turned the second card. "The Tower. You've created a fantasy version of love. The moment reality intrudes, it all comes crashing down."

The woman flushed. "That seems... harsh."

"Then let's see what the Moon says," Lyra continued. "Ah yes. Deception. Delusion. Repeating the same mistake in a new coat."

The woman stood, gathering her purse like she'd just remembered she had somewhere better to be.

"I was told this would be a safe space," she huffed.

Lyra arched one eyebrow. "And I was told that coat was vintage."

The door slammed behind her.

Rowan stared.

Lyra calmly reset her deck.

"I want one," he said.

She looked at him. "A boyfriend by Christmas?"

"No. A reading."

He didn't answer right away.

He was still thinking about the way she'd spoken—calm, precise, like she could see the whole shape of that woman's choices laid out in patterns the rest of them couldn't see. And Rowan wanted to know what his pattern looked like. Not because he thought it'd be good. But because part of him still didn't believe there was one.

He just shrugged. "You're scary accurate. I wanna see what you pull."

Chapter Twelve — The Cards

Lyra tapped the seat across from her, "Sit."

The reading nook was quiet. Tucked in the apothecary's corner like a secret. Books leaned on each other above the booth seat, their spines faded from sun. A string of dried rosemary hung above the window, swaying faintly with the draft. Rowan sat across from her, the old table sticky in one spot from spilled tea and candle wax. He didn't ask what the cards meant. He just waited.
"You're actually doing it?"
"You asked."
She shuffled the deck like she'd done it a thousand times, hands smooth, no theatrics. She didn't ask him what he wanted to know. She just cut the deck.
Three cards, placed face-down between them.
She flipped the first one.
King of Cups.
Then the second.
King of Swords.
Rowan frowned. "That seems... specific."
Lyra didn't reply.
She turned the third card: The Tower.
Her expression didn't change. But the warmth in the room did. Like the fireplace had dimmed slightly—or maybe the air was just holding its breath.
"It means," she said slowly, "you're going to step in something."
Rowan blinked. "That's it?"
        Before he could push, Talia leaned into the room, holding a bundle of herbs and a wooden spoon like a threat. "Grilled cheese or curry? Pick one or get both in the same pot."
"Curry," Lyra said flatly.
"You would," Talia shot back.
"It has flavor. You wouldn't understand."
"I invented flavor."
Rowan glanced back at the cards.
        When he looked up, Lyra was already gathering the deck, calm as ever, as if the Kings and the Tower hadn't meant anything at all.
"I'm not making two things!" Talia shouted from the kitchen.

"Then don't cook for me!" Lyra called back.

Rowan looked between them, slowly sliding the tarot cards out of his immediate reach.

Talia stormed into the doorway holding a wooden spoon like it was a weapon. "You always want something complicated and then criticize the execution."

"I don't criticize," Lyra said evenly. "I observe. And what I observed last time was under-seasoned, overcooked—"

"Say 'grilled cheese crime' one more time, I dare you."

"You served it with a rosemary aioli, Talia. It's a sandwich, not a eulogy." Rowan wasn't sure if the smell coming from the kitchen was curry or scorched pride.

Selene walked past them, entirely unfazed, and poured herself tea like this had happened a thousand times before.

Rowan leaned closer to her. "Do they always fight like this?"

Selene sipped. "Only about important things."

Lyra stood, gathering her coat like a queen abandoning the court. "I'll handle myself today," she announced. "Clearly the culinary standards here have fallen."

"Where are you going?" Talia snapped.

"Out."

"With what food?"

"With my own standards," Lyra said, and then turned to Rowan. "You. Come on. We're eating like gods."

Rowan blinked. "Me?"

"You've earned it."

"Wait, is this a reward or an escape plan?"

"Yes."

Rowan hesitated only for a second.

Then he grabbed his coat and followed.

Rowan followed, though every logical part of him was screaming What are you doing? He didn't know where they were going. He didn't even know if Lyra had a plan. But something about the way she moved—the calm confidence, the complete lack of explanation—made it feel like asking questions would've just slowed her down.

She didn't explain where they were going.

Didn't look back.

Didn't offer so much as a hint.

They walked two blocks in near silence. Rowan matched her pace without asking why, without questioning if this was a terrible idea.

49

It definitely was.

And still, he followed.

The steakhouse came into view like a brick fortress of questionable decisions. Bold lettering. Smoked glass. Faux gas lamps flanking the doors like sentries. A place that took itself seriously—on purpose. Inside, the lighting was low and dramatic. Wood paneling everywhere. Booths like confessionals. The kind of place that assumed anyone under eighteen had to be supervised or exorcised.

Lyra pushed the door open with one hand, held it for Rowan with the other, and strolled inside like she owned the place.

The waitress standing behind the host stand smiled—until she saw who it was.

Her face dropped.

Not in a fearful way.

In a resigned way.

Like someone remembering they were still legally obligated to serve a returning menace.

Rowan didn't know what this place was, but by the way the hostess flinched at Lyra's smile, he was starting to understand.

Chapter Thirteen — The Steakhouse

The steakhouse smelled like smoke, butter, and something sizzling just shy of burning. The floors were dark wood. The booths were deep red leather, cracked at the seams from too many elbows and too much melted cheese. Every table seemed to come with its own ambient cloud of beef and bravado.

Rowan stopped two steps inside the door, blinking against the amber lighting. The scent hit him first—char, grease, something primal. He couldn't tell if it made him hungry or nervous. Maybe both.

There was laughter. Glass clinking. The sharp clatter of plates in the kitchen and a server shouting for more fries like it was a matter of life and death.

Rowan had never been in a place like this before. Maybe once or twice, through the front door of a fast-food place to use the bathroom, but nothing like this. This wasn't "grab a burger and leave."

This was ceremony. Forks clinked. Servers moved like trained performers. Even the napkins were folded like they had purpose. And everyone in here seemed to know the rules but him.

He hovered by the entrance, unsure what to do with his hands. His coat suddenly felt too thin. His boots too loud. He glanced at the door, half-considering stepping back out—

"Relax," Lyra said, already halfway to a booth.

He followed automatically, because trying to keep up with her felt easier than staying still. The waitress met them halfway with a laminated menu in one hand and a fake smile already in place—until she saw Lyra.

Her smile dropped like a curtain.

"Oh. It's you."

Lyra gave a polite nod, like she was being recognized for winning an award. "Table for two."

The waitress didn't argue. Just sighed, turned, and led them deeper into the restaurant.

Rowan leaned in as they walked. "What did you do to this place?"

"I won," Lyra said.

She didn't elaborate.

She didn't need to.

Rowan scanned the menu like it was an exam he hadn't studied for. His eyes jumped past the fancy cuts, the combo platters, and the towering burger stacks until he found a little box in the corner with a cartoon cow next to it.

"Little Buckaroo Meal. "Chicken fingers. Fries. A juice box. $6.99. Perfect.

"I'll take the—"

"No," Lyra said flatly, not even looking up from her menu. "Try again."

Rowan frowned. "What? It's food."

"It's not food," she said, flipping a page. "It's a cry for help in nugget form."

"It's the cheapest thing on here."

"And I'm not letting you order off a menu with a coloring section." The waitress returned, pen in hand, eyes already glazed over like she regretted every life choice that brought her here.

Lyra closed her menu with a crisp snap. "He'll have the ribeye. Medium rare. Double fries. No substitutions."

The waitress blinked. "The—okay. And for you?"

"I'd like the steakhouse challenge," Lyra said proudly.

There was a silence.

The waitress stared at her like she wanted to walk directly into traffic.

"Ma'am, that's—are you serious?"

Lyra just smiled.

"I was here last time," the waitress muttered. "You nearly broke the record and then tried to eat the decorative garnish."

"It was fennel. It's edible."

"It was plastic."

Lyra leaned back, entirely unbothered. "And yet I won."

The waitress scribbled something down with the exhausted fury of a woman who knew she'd be fetching an emergency milkshake before this was over.

She walked away without another word.

Rowan stared across the table.

Lyra sipped her water and said, "You're going to eat like you've never eaten steak before."

"I haven't."

"Even better."

The waitress arrived with a cart, and Rowan's jaw nearly hit the table.

Lyra's steak wasn't just big—it had it's own gravity. A 72oz slab of beef, so thick it looked like they'd just removed it from a live cow and slapped it on the plate. The meat was surrounded by a baked potato that was actually big enough to be a meal in itself, drenched in sour cream and chives. On the side, a salad swimming in dressing, a bread roll that could double as a weapon, and the pièce de résistance: a milkshake so thick, it was practically solid. The waitress set the feast down in front of Lyra with an air of resignation. "One hour. Finish everything, and it's free. No sharing. No breaks."

Lyra didn't even glance at the milkshake or the salad. She just looked at the steak and nodded like she was meeting an old friend. "Start the clock."

The waitress pressed a button, sighed, and walked off, like she'd seen this all before.

Lyra grabbed the steak knife, cutting into the massive slab with the kind of precision you'd expect from someone who didn't have time for nonsense.

The first bite went in without hesitation. The steak barely had time to hit her mouth before it was gone, chewed and swallowed. She cut another piece, this time with her eyes still fixed on the next part of the plate. The steak bled just a little at the edges, juices pooling around the cuts in a way that would've made any chef proud. But Lyra didn't care. She just kept cutting, chewing, swallowing.

It wasn't graceful. It wasn't slow. It was efficient.

She barely chewed, just enough to break through the tough parts, and swallowed the steak like it was nothing. A few people in the restaurant were watching now, mouths slightly open in disbelief as she devoured half the steak in the first five minutes. Rowan stared. He was still eating his own ribeye, but it was like chewing through rubber in comparison.

She was halfway through the potato by the time the first diners had turned their chairs around to face her. She ignored them, her focus entirely on the plate. Bite. Swallow. Cut. Repeat.

The milkshake sat untouched, but the potatoes were gone in seconds. Lyra moved through it like she had no care in the world. The salad was pushed aside, but not before she shoved a few pieces of lettuce into her mouth and chewed twice. Then she turned back to the steak.

The meat didn't last long. She tore through it with the kind of energy that made Rowan feel embarrassed about the speed at which he was eating.

"Are you even chewing?" Rowan asked in awe.

Lyra just grinned between bites. "Waste of time."

The steak was gone in twenty minutes. The plate was empty. The milkshake? Well, that was the last challenge. She grabbed the straw, didn't even bother with the spoon, and slurped it down in a few long swallows.

By the time the waitress returned, Lyra was sitting back, completely unbothered.

The woman stared down at the empty plate. Then at Lyra. Then back at the plate.

"Well," the waitress muttered, "I guess you're done."

Lyra smiled. "Told you."

The entire restaurant seemed to breathe again, like they'd been holding their breath this whole time.

Rowan stared at the last third of his ribeye like it had personally wronged him.

He'd started strong—really, he had. The first few bites had been incredible. But somewhere between the midway point and now, his stomach had issued a ceasefire. Every chew felt heavier. Slower. Like the meat was expanding inside him.

Lyra glanced over, sipping the last of her milkshake like it was nothing. "You done?"

"I'm pacing myself," Rowan mumbled.

She raised an eyebrow. "That steak is pacing you."

He took one more bite out of spite, then put his fork down and leaned back with a defeated sigh.

Without a word, Lyra reached across the table and swiped the remaining fries off his plate. She dipped one into his abandoned sauce and popped it into her mouth like she was sampling hors d'oeuvres at a gallery opening.

Rowan watched her with something between horror and admiration.

"You don't even look full," he said.

"I'm not."

"Where is it going?"

Lyra didn't answer. She just raised one hand lazily as the waitress approached.

"Do you still do the chocolate cake?" she asked.

The waitress gave her a haunted look. "You're not serious."

"Oh, I'm very serious."

A few minutes later, the cake arrived. It wasn't a slice. It was a statement. Dense, glossy, stacked with frosting and unapologetically huge.

Lyra picked up her fork and dove in.

Rowan watched in disbelief as she took bite after bite, completely unfazed.

"You're going to die," he said softly.

Lyra didn't even look up. "Maybe. But I'll die fulfilled."

Chapter Fourteen — Back at the Apothecary

"—and then she ordered cake," Rowan said, hands in the air like he still couldn't believe it. "After the steak. After the fries. After the milkshake."

Talia gasped, both hands over her mouth. "No."

"Oh yes."

"She ordered dessert? After the—after that?"

Rowan nodded solemnly. "And then she ate half my fries. Without blinking."

Selene, seated at the counter with her usual mug of tea, didn't look up. "You didn't stop her."

"I couldn't. I was busy trying to survive."

"I warned you," Elysse said from behind the register. "Taking Lyra to a restaurant is a diplomatic incident waiting to happen."

"She ate a seventy-two-ounce steak in twenty-four minutes," Rowan said, as if recounting a war story. "And then the baked potato. And the milkshake. And the cake. She didn't even look full."

"Where did she put it?" Talia asked.

"Don't ask," Elysse muttered.

Lyra strolled in from the back, unbothered, sipping something out of a glass bottle that definitely wasn't tea.

"I regret nothing," she said, flopping dramatically onto the couch.

"You should regret something," Rowan said.

"Not even a little." she grinned

"You committed a biological miracle. Or a crime. Or both."

Lyra gave him a lazy smile. "You're just jealous I finished your fries."

Rowan opened his mouth to argue—and couldn't. Because he was a little jealous. And also kind of impressed.

He sank onto the stool beside the counter, shaking his head. "That was the best and worst thing I've ever seen."

Talia pointed a spoon at Lyra. "If you die early, it's going to be from your arteries revolting."

Lyra leaned back, eyes closed. "Then I will die as I lived—smug and well-fed."

"So," Selene said mildly, setting her tea aside, "now that the carnage has been relived in full color—"

"It was high-definition carnage," Rowan cut in.

"—we need to rotate the stock for Mother's Day."

Rowan blinked. "Already?"

"It's our second-biggest day of the year," Elysse said. "Behind October third."

"What's October third?"

"The day all the tourists remember we exist."

Talia practically bounced into the room, already rolling up her sleeves. "We need the rose soaps, the jasmine scrubs, the lemon balm balm—don't look at me like that, it's branded—and the 'Mom Deserves Better' candles."

"We're really selling that?" Rowan asked.

"It's our best-seller," Lyra said flatly. "And not just for moms."

Selene handed him a clipboard. "Check the dates and pull anything fresh from the cellar. We'll need a full rotation by tomorrow."

Rowan took the clipboard like it might explode. "Why does the apothecary have a cellar?"

"It's not a dungeon," Elysse said.

"It's absolutely a dungeon," Lyra added.

"It's temperature-controlled," Selene corrected. "And I'm not storing handmade scrubs next to the furnace."

Rowan sighed and stood. "Do I get gloves or am I going to have glitter on me until July?"

"No promises," Talia sang while handing him a pair of too big cloth gloves. One of the fingers had sparkly residue.

"Cool," he muttered. "Love this job."

He disappeared toward the back, the others already following, voices rising into another wave of overlapping tasks and increasingly specific product requests.

Lyra held the door open and called after him, "And if you see a crate labeled 'Cursed Grapefruit,' don't touch it!"

Rowan's voice echoed up the stairs.

"WHY IS THAT EVEN A CATEGORY?!"

The cellar was cool and dry, lined with shelves that looked like they'd been built in the 1800s and never dusted since. Crates were stacked neatly by scent, season, and in at least one case, cryptic symbols that Rowan chose not to ask about.

He worked in silence for a while, cross-checking labels with the clipboard and passing boxes up the stairs.

Lemon verbena. Jasmine rose. Lavender citrus. Each one packaged perfectly. Each one labeled with some gentle variation of "For Mom."

Rowan's rhythm slowed.

He stood there, holding a small box of honey and oat soap with a tag that read Thank you for always being there.

The words hit harder than he expected.

He stared at the label. Just a second too long.

Behind him, footsteps creaked on the stairs.

Selene.

She didn't say anything at first—just moved quietly past him, checking her own section of inventory.

But after a moment, she glanced his way. "You alright?" her voice low and kind.

Rowan didn't look up. "Yeah. Just thinking about the rush."

"Mm." Her voice was soft, but she didn't push. "It'll be busy."

"I can handle it," he said quickly.

"I know you can."

She gave him one more look—gentle, thoughtful—then moved on without comment.

He stood there a few moments longer before shaking it off and lifting the box.

"Let's go ruin some shelves with seasonal color schemes," he muttered—

but he didn't put the soap down.

Chapter Fifteen — The Rush

It started at 9:00 a.m. sharp.

By 9:07, someone had knocked over the seasonal candle display.

By 9:12, a man with a Bluetooth headset had asked if the soaps were "edible."

By 9:18, Rowan had answered the same question—"What scent says 'mother' but also 'forgiveness'?"—four separate times, with decreasing patience.

He didn't know how it had happened, but Mother's Day at the Apothecary was apparently a regional event.

The shop was packed. Packed.

The old wood floors creaked under the rows of visitors squeezed between shelves, sniffing things aggressively, arguing over soap gift bundles like it was an Olympic sport. Someone had opened a scrub jar and was sampling it like frosting. A woman cornered Elysse and demanded to know which bath bomb would best "erase a decade of mistakes."

Talia was near the front window shouting, "If it's pink and floral, we're out! If it's lemon or lavender, grab it now or forever hold your complaints!"

Selene stood behind the register, eerily calm, scanning purchases and gently redirecting chaos like she had a map of it memorized.

Lyra, of course, was pretending not to work at all—curled up in an armchair with a cup of tea, flipping through a magazine, occasionally calling out advice like, "The scrub on the left smells better. You're welcome." She didn't even glance up. Just turned a page with the kind of lazy precision that said she had transcended retail.

Rowan moved through it all like a survivor in a battlefield—holding a clipboard in one hand, restocking soaps with the other.

"I need a refill on citrus balm!" Talia yelled.

"I just brought up five jars!"

"Well, bring more! These people are aggressive and moisturized!"

Rowan ducked behind the counter and wiped his forehead with the back of his wrist. "This is insane."

Elysse passed him a bag of wrapped soaps and didn't miss a beat. "This is Mother's Day."

Rowan pushed the latest crate of soaps through the back door, bracing it with one foot before it could get yanked away again.

Three customers were already waiting for him.

"Lavender?"

"Is that the jasmine blend?"

"Oh my god, are those the mango-rose?"

He barely managed to set the crate down before they were reaching in—grabbing bars straight from the box, digging through the packing paper like seagulls attacking an open bag of chips.

"Can I get a fresh one?"

"These look like they were stacked too tightly—this one's dented!"

"I saw her grab two—she grabbed two!"

Rowan just backed up, hands raised, expression deadpan. "By all means, help yourselves."

He turned, took three steps toward the cellar, and someone called, "When do you restock the body oils?"

"In fifteen minutes," he said without looking.

"You said that fifteen minutes ago!"

"Then I'm consistent."

He ducked down the stairs and exhaled hard as soon as the door swung shut behind him.

It was cooler down there. Quieter. Blessedly free of screaming pastel gift bags and customers trying to fistfight over floral soap.

He grabbed another box, pried it open, and caught the faint scent of lavender curling up from the top layer.

Warm. Clean. Gentle.

He hesitated—just a second—then reached in and slipped a single bar into his coat pocket. Like someone had tried to bottle kindness and got surprisingly close.

Didn't think about it.

Didn't say anything.

Just... took it.

Then he picked up the box and carried it back upstairs like nothing had happened.

The last customer left at 6:58 p.m., dragging a floral-scented tote and muttering about exfoliation as she went.

Rowan flipped the little "Open" sign to "Closed" with something close to reverence.

The store was wrecked.

Half the displays were picked over. Glitter clung to the floorboards like it had declared squatters' rights. Talia was lying flat on the rug behind the counter, arm draped dramatically over her face.

"We made it," she groaned. "Tell my story."

60

"I'll carve it into your headstone," Elysse muttered, counting receipts.

Selene locked the register and looked around. "Alright. Quick reset tomorrow. Everyone get some rest."

Rowan started sweeping near the back, still riding the low hum of exhaustion. His hands were dry from all the boxes, his feet ached, and somehow he still smelled like lemongrass.

The bell above the door chimed.

And everything stilled.

Not quiet. Not silent. Still. The scent of rosewater and sandalwood, too crisp for the season, followed him in like a shadow.

The air didn't go cold. It went flat.

Elysse's pen froze in midair.

"Lucian," she said under her breath.

A man stepped inside—clean lines, dark suit, hair neatly styled like he'd walked out of a portrait and into reality. No coat, despite the chill. No rush, no hesitation. He moved like someone who didn't need to explain himself.

Rowan looked up—and stopped. Something in his ribs tightened, like his body recognized danger before his mind caught up.

The man's eyes flicked to him first. Just briefly. Just long enough.

Selene's smile didn't reach her eyes. "Lucian."

"Closing already?" Lucian said smoothly, voice like warm glass.

Talia didn't sit up.

Lyra didn't look away from her tea.

Elysse froze mid-count, jaw tightening just slightly.

Lucian stepped further into the room, surveying the chaos like a museum exhibit.

"I was in the area," he said. "Thought I'd drop in."

Rowan took half a step back before he realized he was doing it.

Lucian's eyes slid toward him again.

Just for a moment.

Just enough to make it feel personal.

61

Chapter Sixteen-The Visit

Lucian Aubrey did not enter, he arrived.

Even standing still, he seemed to take up more space than he should. The room adjusted to him—the lighting, the air, the temperature of every unspoken thing.

Rowan didn't move.

He just stood there, broom still in hand, watching the man who had stepped into their shop like it belonged to him.

He was tall—impossibly so in the doorway—broad-shouldered in a perfectly tailored charcoal coat, the kind that whispered wealth instead of shouting it. His hair was ink-black, combed back like a slick blade, not a strand out of place. Sharp cheekbones. Unsmiling mouth. His skin had that ageless, too-smooth quality that made Rowan unsure if he was thirty-five or a hundred and thirty-five. His eyes—light gray, almost silver—didn't just look *at* you. They sifted. Measured.

Lucian studied him openly. Not coldly. Not cruelly. Just... precisely.

His gaze moved from Rowan's shoulders to his jaw, to the faint scuff on his left boot, to the bar of lavender soap still poking out of his coat pocket.

"You've grown," Lucian said, like he was confirming a hypothesis.

Rowan didn't answer.

Because somehow, he knew who this man was—even if no one had told him yet. Not so much in words but in Lyra's guarded body language, the way that Elysse had closed her notebook, and even how Selene stood a little straighter.

In the way no one else had spoken since he entered.

Lucian's eyes softened a fraction, though they never lost that surgical edge. "I see they've put you to work."

Rowan said nothing.

Selene moved closer, not touching Rowan, but standing just near enough to signal it.

"He's part of the household now," she said, voice calm but layered. "Not a curiosity to examine."

Lucian didn't take his eyes off Rowan. "He's more than that."

Rowan finally spoke. Quiet. Even.

"I'm right here."

Lucian smiled. "Yes. You are."

Lucian stepped forward.

Not fast. Not threatening.

But deliberate.

Selene shifted instantly, moving between them with the kind of grace that only looked casual if you didn't know better.

"Don't," she said.

Just one word.

But it landed like a command.

Lucian paused—then raised both hands in a slow, measured gesture.

"I swear," he said calmly, "by my power, I will not harm him."

She didn't move. But her eyes didn't leave Rowan.

She was watching for something. Analyzing Lucian's every movement and allowing him to think he was in control. This wasn't fear, it was cold strategy.

Time didn't stop.

But it tightened.

Rowan felt it without knowing why—like the air itself acknowledged something sacred had just been invoked.

No one spoke.

Even Lyra had gone still, watching with unreadable eyes from her seat in the corner.

Selene didn't move, but she gave the faintest nod.

Permission. Conditional.

Lucian stepped forward and lowered himself onto one knee.

A king, in posture if not in name.

He looked Rowan in the eye—not with warmth, not with cruelty, but with impossible calm.

"You're being well cared for," Lucian said softly. "That's... good."

Rowan narrowed his eyes. "You say that like you had anything to do with it."

Lucian smiled, just barely. "Not yet."

Something about that answer made Rowan's stomach knot.

Not from fear, but from the weight of being noticed by someone who always has a plan.

Lucian tilted his head slightly, gaze scanning Rowan's face as if he were studying a painting up close. Then, without warning, he moved.

His hand came up fast—precise—and took Rowan's chin with an unsettling kind of calm. Not tight. Not threatening. But inarguable.

63

Rowan flinched, too stunned to pull away. The touch wasn't rough. It wasn't warm either. It was clinical. Like being examined. Or adjusted. "Hey—" he started.

Then came the heat. A strange pressure bloomed along his gums—too fast, too focused to be natural. Not fire, not pain. Just a ripple of wrongness moving under the surface.

By the time Selene reached them, her fingers closing hard around Lucian's wrist, it was already done.

Rowan jerked back a step, his hand going to his mouth instinctively.

His teeth felt— smooth... and clean. Like they'd been written into his mouth. I should have felt like a gift, but it was tainted by the thought of what else Lucian might have done instead.

He ran his tongue along the edge of them. Whole as if he'd never had a cavity or injury. They were even perfectly aligned.

His breath caught.

Lucian rose slowly, brushing a non-existent wrinkle from his coat sleeve. "You'll find it more comfortable now," he said, like he'd offered directions or passed along a weather report.

Selene's voice was a warning wrapped in steel. "You had no right —"

"I swore not to harm him," Lucian replied, gaze still on Rowan. "You'll find I kept that promise."

Rowan looked at him—this immaculate stranger who'd just reached into his body and changed something without permission —and felt a flicker of something colder than fear. Like he'd been claimed.

Selene let go of Lucian's wrist slowly, but her hand hovered close, magic just under her skin.

Lucian didn't leave. Not yet. He simply stood there, admiring his own restraint. Cold eyes focused on Rowan, curious to see what the boy would do next.

Rowan barely had time to process the foreign feeling in his mouth when Lucian's hand moved again.

Smooth as silk, he reached into Rowan's coat pocket and plucked out the bar of lavender soap.

Rowan tensed. He hadn't even remembered it was there.

Lucian turned it over in his hand, inspecting it like an art piece. "Ah," he murmured. "Lavender."

He looked past Rowan—straight at Selene.

"It's still your favorite, isn't it?"

Selene didn't answer. Her expression didn't shift. But something behind her eyes sparked like flint.

Lucian smiled.

He tossed the soap lightly, underhand, and she caught it without looking down.

"Happy Mother's Day," he said with a cruel and elegant grin.

Then he turned on his heel and walked out, as if he hadn't just walked into their sanctuary, laid hands on her child, and left a calling card behind.

The door shut gently behind him.

The silence he left behind was immediate.

Rowan's jaw tightened—his teeth unfamiliar in his own mouth. He opened his mouth to speak then closed it. He looked to Selene as if she would have the answer. She simple reached over and placed a hand gently on his shoulder "never again" she said softly.

Chapter Seventeen — Fallout

Selene's hands were already on his face. Gentle. Focused. Magic just beneath her fingertips. "Did he hurt you?" she asked. "Rowan, did he do anything else?"

"I'm okay," he said, voice stiff. "It didn't hurt."

"They're just... there now," he said. He didn't know whether to be grateful or violated. All he knew was they felt perfect. Too perfect; like someone had erased the evidence they were ever broken.

She tilted his chin slightly, eyes scanning for any sign of lingering energy, damage, anything she could undo.

"I won't let him touch you again," she said, more to herself than to him. "Next time, I won't wait for a promise."

"I didn't even see him move," Rowan muttered. He could still feel it though. Somewhere deeper. Like an echo had settled in his bones and was waiting to be noticed.

Talia hovered nearby, tense and unusually silent. Elysse was pacing with a notebook in one hand and no intention of writing anything down. Even Lyra had gone still, watching Rowan like he might flicker or vanish.

He rubbed his jaw, still adjusting to the odd, perfect smoothness of it.

"They're fixed," he said. "Like—actually fixed. Even the ones that were pulled. They're just... there now."

Selene's hands dropped. Her expression didn't change, but something in her eyes went cold.

"Who was that guy?" Rowan asked.

Immediately the tension in the room thickened. No one answered right away; they simply looked to each other, silently deciding who would be the one to say it first..

Selene took a breath, slow and careful. "That was Lucian," she said. "Lucian Aubrey." The name felt like a warning label someone had peeled off and slapped back on crooked. She let the name settle before adding, "Arguably the most powerful warlock alive."

Rowan blinked. "Cool." Then, flatly: "So I just got magically orthodontic'd by a demigod."

Lyra flopped back onto the couch with a dramatic groan. "He's also the most exhausting person alive. Shows up all polished

66

and brooding like he's auditioning to play himself in a movie he financed."

"He's not exhausting," Elysse said without looking up. "He's calculated." She set her notebook down and folded her hands in her lap.

"Lucian doesn't do anything without a purpose. Not a visit, not a word, and definitely not a spell. Whatever he did to you— whatever he wanted from seeing you in person—it was part of something bigger."

Rowan frowned. "Bigger than fixing my teeth?"

"Everything with him is bigger," Selene said. "Power isn't the endgame. It's the tool."

"Fantastic," Rowan muttered. "So I'm a... what? Pawn?"

"No," Selene said gently. "You're a child." Rowan's shoulders had curled inward without him realizing, as if bracing for something sharp. His hands twisted together in his lap, the knuckles pale.

"My child."

The words hit like warmth breaking through frost. Rowan's chest tightened, a rush of heat climbing his throat before he could stop it. He blinked hard, but the sting in his eyes betrayed him.

Even Lyra didn't offer a comeback.

Rowan stared at Selene.

She hadn't raised her voice. She hadn't made a declaration. She'd just said it.

Not "you're like family." Not "we're here for you." Just... my child. The words rested like a hand on a door that hadn't been knocked on in a long time.

He didn't know what to do with that. Not in the moment. Maybe not ever.

He blinked once. Twice.

Then—

Talia clapped her hands, startling everyone. "Well! Let's just hope fixing your teeth doesn't come back to bite him."

Lyra groaned audibly. "Talia."

"No! No, come on, that was good! He messed with the bite and now he'll get bitten!"

Rowan blinked again, startled, then—choked on a laugh.

A real one. Quick and sharp and barely held in.

Selene exhaled softly, the tension easing from her shoulders just a little.

Lyra flopped back dramatically. "If puns are your coping mechanism now, I'm leaving."

"You were already sitting."

"I'll sit angrily."

Elysse pinched the bridge of her nose. "Can we focus, please?"

"Can we ever?" Lyra muttered.

Rowan sat back, still stunned—but no longer frozen.

And somewhere deep in his chest, the smallest thread of relief unraveled.

Selene turned to him once more, the worst of the tension drained from her posture.

She opened her hand and held up the lavender soap Lucian had tossed her. "Thank you," she said softly.

Rowan blinked. "I didn't—"

"You did."

She tucked it away, almost gently. "That's why it matters."

She tucked it into her coat pocket, the scent of lavender clung faintly to her.

Rowan didn't say anything. He just nodded.

It wasn't much.

But somehow, it felt like enough.

Selene looked around at the others. "Alright. Let's go home."

Talia groaned and rolled off the rug like she was melting.

Lyra dumped the last of her tea in the sink with flair.

Elysse shut the ledger with a soft thunk.

And Rowan followed them out, teeth still strange in his mouth, but something in his chest just a little steadier than before.

Chapter Eighteen — The Line

Rowan sat at the kitchen table with a notebook open in front of him. The overhead light buzzed faintly. A pot of something herbal steeped on the stove, releasing steam that smelled like mint and something darker beneath. The kitchen window showed a gray sky, flat and cold against the glass.

Not a spellbook this time. No candle stubs or runes or potion ingredients. Just notes. Questions. A lesson written in Elysse's tidy, no-nonsense handwriting.

Across from him, she stirred her tea once, set the spoon aside, and folded her hands like this was any other school day.

It wasn't.

"There's a story in there," she said. "A record, really. Of a mage council that existed before the Cataclysm. Do you know what that was?"

Rowan flipped a page. "Yeah. One of the old world-breaking events. Magic spiraled out of control. Entire regions collapsed."

"They called themselves architects," Elysse said. "Not soldiers. Not tyrants. They weren't cruel by nature. Just... efficient."

He frowned. "Why are we talking about them?"

"Because they used their magic to decide who got to live. Who was 'useful.' Who deserved to remain in the world they were reshaping."

Rowan's jaw tightened. "Did anyone stop them?"

Elysse's expression didn't flicker. "By the time anyone realized what they were doing, half the damage was already done. The rest only stopped because the backlash nearly destroyed them too."

He looked down at the page again. It didn't read like horror. It read like strategy. Cold, quiet, deliberate.

"They didn't think they were the bad guys," Rowan said. "They didn't even realize it until after the damage was done."

"No one ever does." Elysse said softly.

Rowan stared at the page, uncomfortable. The story was colder than anything he'd read in spellbooks. At least magic had warmth, had spark. But this was clinical, almost hollow.

He glanced up. "What does this have to do with me?"

Elysse's eyes softened, just slightly. She'd been expecting the question.

"You have a lot of magic, Rowan. More than we initially thought. More than most witches or warlocks your age."

Rowan looked away. "I know that. I'm training."

"I don't mean your skill level," she said quietly. "I mean your potential. Lightning magic isn't subtle—it's powerful, destructive if misused. Magic like yours can rewrite boundaries, sometimes permanently."

He swallowed. "So you think I might end up like them?"

"No," Elysse said firmly. "Because you ask that question."

Rowan hesitated, pencil tapping softly against the notebook's edge.

"But Lucian doesn't," she continued. "Lucian Aubrey believes he's above those questions. He sees power as a right—not a responsibility."

Rowan stilled, remembering the calm, invasive touch that fixed his teeth without permission.

"He thinks he knows better," Rowan murmured.

Elysse nodded. "And he has convinced himself that everything he does is justified. No anger, no hate—just efficiency. Just like the architects."

Rowan's throat felt tight. He flipped the notebook closed, avoiding Elysse's careful gaze. "So what's supposed to stop me from becoming him?"

Elysse didn't flinch. She'd clearly been waiting for exactly this moment.

"You," she said. "Because unlike Lucian, you understand there's a line. And you're asking where it is."

Rowan sat quietly, eyes focused somewhere past Elysse's shoulder. "He didn't even threaten me," Rowan finally said, voice low. "Lucian. He just acted like it was normal. Like... fixing me was a favor."

Elysse nodded. "That's what makes him dangerous. He's not trying to control people—he thinks he's correcting them. Like rearranging furniture in a room that isn't his."

Rowan's hand curled into a loose fist. "How can someone so powerful be that disconnected?"

"It happens gradually," Elysse replied softly. "He's lived a long time, and he stopped seeing people as people. Now they're problems, obstacles, tools—something to rearrange, not understand."

Rowan was silent. He thought of the strange, detached gentleness Lucian had used, how casually he'd taken control. He thought of his own magic—the sparks that sometimes came faster and stronger than intended.

"So how do you stop it?" he asked. "How do you know you're not going too far?"

Elysse's expression softened. "You ask. You pay attention. You stay uncomfortable with using power as convenience. That hesitation you feel? That discomfort? That's not weakness. It's your best protection."

Rowan stared at the closed notebook, the quiet truth settling around him.

Elysse stood slowly, resting a reassuring hand on his shoulder. "Magic itself isn't dangerous. What matters is who's using it, and why. Lucian forgot that a long time ago. But you're just beginning." She gave his shoulder a gentle squeeze. "Keep asking questions. That's how you'll always know where the line is."

Rowan stayed at the table long after Elysse had gone back to the front room.

He stared at the closed notebook, tapping his pencil lightly against the cover, lost in thought.

It wasn't the lesson he'd expected today—but it was the one he'd needed.

Magic was powerful. Magic was tempting. Magic could make life easier, smoother, effortless. But that ease came at a price—one that couldn't be paid in dollars or gold.

It cost something much harder to regain once it was lost: humanity.

He thought again of Lucian, of that brief, invasive moment when the older man had reached out and touched him without hesitation. Lucian hadn't asked permission; he hadn't hesitated or explained. Because, in Lucian's mind, he didn't need to. Rowan had been something to improve, something to adjust.

Something convenient.

A quiet shiver moved down Rowan's spine.

No. Lucian wasn't gone. He'd made his intentions perfectly clear: Rowan was someone he intended to keep an eye on.

That first encounter wasn't a coincidence—it was a promise.

Lucian Aubrey would return, calm, powerful, reasonable—and the next time, it would be more than just an adjustment. It would be an offer, maybe even a demand.

And Rowan would have to choose; not what he could do, but what he *should*.

He took a slow, steady breath, finally opening his notebook again. At the very bottom of the page, he wrote one sentence in neat, careful handwriting:
There has to be a line—and I have to hold it.

Chapter Nineteen — Control

Summer crept into Ashford Landing like a cat that owned the place.

The breeze was warm and aimless. The flower boxes out front had started to wilt from heat and boredom. Tourists came less often, and when they did, they stayed just long enough to complain about the humidity before wandering off in search of ice cream or air conditioning.

The apothecary was quiet.

Not abandoned—just... still.

The scent of dried herbs clung to the walls. The inventory stayed stocked, untouched. Candles burned a little slower, spells took their time.

It was the in-between season.

Spring had been chaos. Fall would be busier still. But summer? Summer felt like it forgot to bring a purpose.

Which made it dangerous.

Because people got lazy in summer. They mistook heat for rest. But Selene didn't believe in rest.

And neither, now, did Rowan.

Rowan hit the ground with a solid thud. His shirt, damp with sweat, clung to his back. Dust streaked his arms, and a rip near one knee exposed the smudged skin beneath—twelve, scrappy, and still growing into clothes that never quite fit right. Dust exploded around him. A few stray sparks crackled along the grass where he'd landed, fading as quickly as they came.

"Again," Lyra called. The grass behind the apothecary had been trampled into uneven patches—some green, some scorched, a few charred completely bare. Old training dummies leaned against the fence like they'd survived a small war. A chalk ring, half-faded, marked where Selene insisted they spar "with intention." It smelled faintly of ozone, sweat, and whatever magic didn't quite burn clean.

Rowan groaned into the dirt. "Define again."

"Define standing," she shot back.

He rolled over, scowling, and wiped his forearm across his forehead. The summer heat clung to everything—skin, breath, clothes—and Lyra was somehow still bone-dry, looking like she hadn't broken a sweat in hours.

She stood a few yards away, arms crossed, a smirk playing at the corner of her mouth. Her boots left scorched grass where she'd pivoted. Her magic hummed beneath the surface like a live wire wrapped in sarcasm. Her long hair pulled into a warriors braid. A streak of ash clung to one cheek but her expression was coll as ever; like summer was something that happened to other people.

"I'm not even trying to win," Rowan muttered.

"You're failing perfectly," she replied cheerfully. "Which means we can build from here."

He pushed himself to his feet, jaw tight. "I'm better at precision."

"Precision's for paperwork. This is lightning."

She raised a hand.

A sharp crack filled the air—and Rowan barely dodged the burst of static that sizzled past his ear.

"Reflexes!" Lyra called. "Come on, Blue Eyes! Hit me like you mean it!"

Rowan exhaled sharply, hands up now, energy coiling under his skin.

This wasn't about aiming candles or tapping into quiet thoughts.

This was movement. Power. Lightning.

And Lyra was more than ready to remind him what happens when you hold back.

Lyra didn't wait for him to catch his breath.

She turned on her heel, crossed to the edge of the training yard, and grabbed a thick block of wood from the pile beside the shed.

"Watch closely," she said.

Rowan barely had time to register what she was holding before her fist connected.

CRACK.

The wood didn't snap.

It splintered—clean down the middle. Like paper.

Rowan blinked. "That was enchanted, wasn't it?"

"Nope."

"You're lying."

"I'm better than you."

And then she was coming at him.

Same stance. Same momentum. Same raised fist.

Rowan braced himself—but something in her movement, something in the angle, screamed this one won't miss.

His body moved before he did.

Too fast.

He pivoted, dropped low, and rolled to the left—clean out of the strike zone—just as her punch whistled past where his shoulder had been.

He came up on one knee, breathing hard, every hair on his arms standing up.

Lyra straightened slowly.

"...Interesting," she said.

"What was that?" Rowan panted.

"You tell me."

"I—I just moved."

"Mm." Her voice was calm now. Measured. Curious.

"That wasn't lightning," she added. "That wasn't luck."

Rowan blinked.

"What was it?"

Lyra's eyes narrowed slightly—not angry. Just studying.

"That," she said, "looked a lot like celerity."

Rowan stood slowly, still catching his breath.

The air around him felt... thinner. Like something had torn through it and hadn't quite stitched itself back together.

"Celerity?" he asked. "What even is that?"

Lyra didn't smirk this time.

She crossed her arms, expression flattening into something quiet and serious.

"It's not speed," she said. "Not really. It's time distortion."

Rowan blinked. "That sounds worse."

"It is."

She nodded toward where he'd dodged. "To you, it felt like reflexes. Movement. But to me, it looked like the world stuttered and you slid through the gap."

Rowan didn't respond. His brain was still catching up.

"Celerity doesn't just let you move fast," she went on. "It lets you decide how fast time feels around you. A blade swings, and you move before it starts. A spell casts, and you're already gone."

He stared at her. "That's—"

"—exactly what makes Lucian so dangerous." she confirmed.

The name landed heavy.

Lyra nodded, not looking away. "He's the only warlock we've ever seen with celerity. And paired with his biokinesis..."

Rowan felt the ghost of that pressure again—the heat under his skin, the strange, painless adjustment of his bones.

"—he doesn't need to fight," she finished. "He can dodge anything. He can reach you before you realize he's moved. And if he touches you, he can rewrite you from the inside out."

Rowan was silent.

Lyra let that sit for a second longer, then added, more quietly now: "You just moved like him."

Rowan's stomach sank. Not because of what he could do.

But because of who else could do it.

Lyra tilted her head, eyes narrowing slightly.

"Alright," she said, more to herself than to him. "We'll have to double down."

Rowan blinked. "Double down on what?"

"Your drills. Your focus. Your balance work. Maybe resistance training. Definitely timing exercises. You'll need precision control if you're going to slip between seconds like that."

Rowan stared at her, horrified. "I don't even know what that means."

"Oh, you will."

"No. No, see, I was already getting thrown across the yard by lightning. That was already bad."

Lyra was pacing now, muttering to herself. "I'll have to make the targets move. Or make you move. Possibly both."

"Lyra."

"Maybe training in the cellar. Less space to cheat time."

"Lyra."

She stopped and grinned.

Rowan groaned. "I hate my life."

"Good. That means it's working."

He flopped dramatically onto the grass. "I'd like to go back to the part where I was just weird and angry."

"Oh, honey," she said sweetly, "you're still all those things."

She clapped her hands once. "Alright! Break's over. Up."

"I just discovered a new form of magic. Can't I have, like, a cookie?"

"No," Lyra said. "But I'll let you dodge another punch."

Rowan groaned again—but stood.

Because somehow, even while hating it, he knew she was right.

Getting stronger wasn't a threat, it was a semblance of control.

Chapter Twenty — No Accidents

The moment Rowan tapped into celerity, everything changed.

No one said it directly. No one told him you're dangerous now, or we're worried you'll turn into Lucian; but Elysse cut his school hours in half.

Selene reduced his shifts at the apothecary, and somehow—somehow—Talia was now involved with his training. That part might have been worse than all the others.

"This is a strength exercise," she said cheerfully, dumping a canvas bag of bricks into his arms.

Rowan staggered. "This is a test of faith". He adjusted the weight, boots digging into the sun-warmed dirt, arms trembling under the load. The bricks shifted slightly in the bag, and Rowan silently promised whatever god was listening that if he survived this, he was never helping anyone move apartments. Ever.

Talia beamed. "Good instincts! You're going to need those."

Every morning now began with drills.

If he wasn't sparring with Lyra, he was running footwork drills with Talia—who made them feel like a dance-off and a demolition derby at the same time. If Selene had her way, he was meditating in the garden and trying not to collapse into the bushes. And Elysse?

She wasn't pulling punches either.

"You're not just training magic," she told him flatly. "You're learning how to choose it."

Because celerity wasn't like the others.

It didn't manifest with emotion. It didn't respond to willpower or raw intent.

It surfaced when the stakes were immediate.

When time bent for you—and dared you to misuse it.

Rowan squinted at the training dummy like it had insulted his ancestors.

Nothing happened.

He narrowed his stance. Flexed his fingers. Focused.

Still nothing.

Talia leaned on the garden gate, holding an apple she had absolutely no intention of sharing. A bee hummed lazily past his ear. The garden's heat buzzed, thick with rosemary and the distant scent of sun-warmed soap. Somewhere behind the trellis, a windchime gave a half-hearted jingle, like even it was too tired to fully commit. "You gonna blink it into submission, or...?"

"I'm trying to trigger it," Rowan muttered. "It just—won't come when I call it."

"Have you considered threatening it?"

Rowan shot her a look.

She shrugged. "Worked for my first boyfriend."

He took a breath, tried again. Movement. Intent. Focus. Nothing.

"It only happens when I'm in danger," he said, frustrated. "When something's about to hit me."

Talia's eyes lit up in a way that made Rowan immediately regret saying anything.

"No."

"You don't even know what I was going to say."

"You were going to throw something at me."

She looked offended. "I was going to throw several things at you."

He groaned. "There has to be a safer way."

Talia took a bite of her apple. "Safety is not how you train lightning time magic."

Rowan paced back, then forward, then groaned again and dragged his hands down his face.

"I hate this."

"You say that every day," she said sweetly. "And every day, you get a little faster."

He sighed, looked up at the sky like it might save him, and muttered, "I miss algebra."

Talia tossed the apple core and cracked her knuckles.

"Dodge ball it is."

The second Selene stepped through the garden gate, Rowan ran for her like she was the last glass of water in a desert made entirely of chaos and dodgeballs.

"Please," he gasped. "Make them stop."

Selene raised one brow as he skidded to a halt in front of her.

He was flushed, sweat-slicked, hair sticking up in three directions. There was a smudge of dirt on his cheek, a bruise blooming on his elbow, and one of his sleeves was mysteriously scorched.

She looked him over once

"I see training went well."

"They're monsters."
Selene reached out and gently tucked his collar back into place, brushing a bit of grass off his shoulder.
"You're doing fine."
"I almost got hit with a cast iron skillet."
"That sounds like Talia."
"I dodged it!" he added, as if that made it better.
Selene smiled softly. "Then the training's working."
Rowan blinked. "That's not the point. I'm tired. I'm bruised. I can't feel my legs."
She gave his arm a light squeeze.
"Don't be late for dinner."

And with that, she turned and walked into the house—leaving Rowan standing in the middle of the garden, betrayed by the only adult he thought might have mercy.
...This family is insane," he muttered.
From somewhere behind the herb wall, Talia shouted, "We heard that!"

Rowan had stopped feeling his arms sometime after the third "spontaneous" agility test. His shirt clung to him like regret, and every joint in his body felt like it had been personally hexed by Talia's enthusiasm.
But he'd kept going. Because part of him was afraid of what would happen if he didn't. Not punishment—but disappointment. And that was worse.

By the time dinner was laid out, Rowan could barely remember why he'd ever complained about anything.

Selene hadn't just cooked—she'd prepared a feast, the kind of meal usually reserved for special occasions or quiet holidays when no tourists disturbed the town. It was her way of silently acknowledging the extra demands his training had placed on him, even if she'd never admit it aloud.

The dining table creaked under the weight of heavy ceramic dishes. There was crispy fried chicken, perfectly golden and tender beneath a crunchy seasoned crust; buttery mashed potatoes, whipped until impossibly smooth and topped with a river of savory brown gravy; and fresh-baked dinner rolls, brushed generously with melted butter so they gleamed softly beneath the kitchen lights.

Beside that were platters of roasted vegetables—carrots glazed with honey and thyme, green beans cooked down slowly with smoked bacon, and sweet corn that tasted like late summer evenings. The comforting aroma of macaroni and cheese, creamy and bubbling beneath a crispy breadcrumb crust, filled the dining room, mingling with the gentle spice of a pot of slow-simmered collard greens.

Rowan's eyes widened when he realized she'd even made sweet potato casserole, dotted with brown sugar and toasted pecans, caramelized and fragrant.

"You made all this?" Rowan asked, voice heavy with astonishment —and maybe just a little awe.

Selene placed one last dish—a deep pan of peach cobbler, crust baked to a golden perfection—at the center of the table, her expression serene and unbothered. "You're training hard. You need proper fuel."

"He trains every day!" Talia pointed out, loading her plate. "So, you'll just have to cook like this forever."

"I'm aware," Selene said, calmly handing Rowan an extra-large plate. "Eat."

Rowan didn't argue, filling his plate until there was barely space to hold it. As he began to eat—first slow, savoring the rich flavors, then faster as hunger overtook him—he realized something important:

Selene didn't fuss. She didn't smother. Instead, she simply made sure no one at her table ever walked away hungry. That was her way—steady, quiet, and generous enough to leave no doubt.

He glanced at her, and for a second, he swore he saw a small, satisfied smile.

Then she just said, gently, "There's plenty more in the kitchen."

Talia retold the story of Rowan nearly running into the chicken coop at "unholy speed," complete with sound effects. Lyra threw a roll at her halfway through for dramatic exaggeration. Elysse muttered something about documenting the trajectory in her notes.

Rowan said nothing for most of it—too busy chewing and trying not to fall asleep in his mashed potatoes.

Selene finally sat down last, carrying the pot of stew and a small plate of sliced pears. She looked across the table at Rowan, who was half-slumped in his chair but still lifting his fork like a champion.

"You kept up," she said.

He grunted something halfway between thank you and please don't make me do it again.

Talia raised her glass. "To our little lightning bolt!"

"Who can now dodge cast iron!" Lyra added, clinking her cup against Talia's.

Rowan just mumbled, "I hate you all," into his plate.

"You'll hate us more in fall," Elysse said casually, cutting into her food.

Rowan blinked. "What happens in fall?"

The table went quiet for exactly one beat too long.

Then Talia grinned.

"Oh, sweet summer child."

Selene just smiled faintly and passed him the bread basket.

"Eat up," she said. "You'll need your strength."

Chapter Twenty-One — Fall Rush

The first leaf hadn't even hit the ground yet when the storm began—one paper sign in the window, three boxes marked "Seasonal Emergency," and suddenly it was fall, whether the town agreed or not.

Rowan had survived summer.

Barely.

He had the bruises, scorch marks, and muscle definition to prove it.

But nothing—nothing—could've prepared him for autumn prep at the Apothecary.

The chaos hit like a seasonal curse.

"I need the pumpkin molds!" Talia shouted from the back room.

"Which set?" Rowan called.

"The big ones! And the tiny ones! But not the medium ones, they look indecisive!"

He blinked. "Okay. Sure. That's a thing."

Lyra slid past him holding two boxes labeled FALL FLAVORS - DO NOT OPEN UNLESS YOU WANT REGRET.

"You don't want to know," she muttered, catching his stare.

Elysse was reorganizing shelves with military precision. "Cinnamon bundles go to the left of the window, not the right. Lighting angles affect the spell activation."

"That's not a real thing," Rowan said.

Elysse looked at him over her glasses. "Do you want to explode your eyebrows again?"

He shut up and moved the bundles.

The front room looked like a pumpkin spice storm had hit full force. Candles in every size and color. Baskets of leaf-stamped soaps. Spells for good luck, cozy dreams, and curse reversals disguised as wax melts.

Selene stood near the counter like a calm eye in the storm, sipping tea, completely unaffected by the chaos she herself had scheduled.

"You could've warned me," Rowan muttered as he passed her with an armful of dried orange peels.

"I thought about it," she said.

Rowan stared into the open bin in front of him like it might bite.

Inside: felt pumpkins with glittery eyes, ceramic black cats wearing tiny scarves, LED acorns, and what appeared to be a stack of "Charmed Autumn" window clings in four different fonts.

"...What is this," he asked.

Lyra didn't even look up. "Decorations."

"No, I got that part. Why are they like this?"

Talia popped her head around the shelf with a garland of fake maple leaves draped around her neck. "Because if we don't, Mayor Trent will smite us with a clipboard and passive-aggressive newsletters."

Rowan blinked. "Wait, like—the mayor?"

"Yes," Elysse said flatly, from somewhere under a box labeled PUMPKIN STUFF - TRENT APPROVED.

"He's obsessed with the tourist season," Lyra added. "Has a whole checklist of fall expectations for every business in Ashford Landing. If your storefront doesn't look like a pumpkin patch threw up on it, you get a warning."

"And then a fine," Elysse said.

"And then," Talia said with far too much drama, "he visits personally."

Rowan stared at them.

"No one's seen him eat," Talia whispered. "I'm just saying."

"You're telling me if we don't over-decorate, the mayor comes to yell at us?"

"No," Selene said calmly, stepping in from the back. "He doesn't yell."

Rowan raised a brow.

"He... monologues."

A chill ran down Rowan's spine. "Oh gods, that's worse."

"Much," Selene agreed.

Talia slapped a glittery bat sticker on Rowan's chest. "So grab a scarecrow, rookie. We've got a window to violate."

Rowan was halfway through detangling a string of plastic jack-o'-lantern lights when he asked, "So... what happens if you decorate too much?" The lights buzzed faintly in his hands, glowing orange even though they weren't plugged in

The room paused.

Talia stopped mid-garland.

Elysse closed her labeling book, very slowly.

Even Selene looked up.

Lyra, grinning like she'd been waiting all day for this, leaned on the counter. "You mean the year we broke the town?"

"Oh no," Rowan muttered.

"Oh yes," she said. "We went all in. Fog machines. Timed sound effects. We used enchantments—subtle ones, glamored—so it all passed as 'clever lighting' and 'good production.' Whispering floorboards, glowing bottles, a haunted herb wall."

"You made a child cry," Elysse reminded her.

"Atmosphere is a risk," Lyra said, unbothered.

"They thought we were an actual haunted house," Talia added. "People came in expecting candles and left in a panic when the animatronic skeleton in the corner said, 'Welcome, sinner.'"

Rowan stared. "That wasn't magical?"

"Technically, no," Lyra said. "We just... enhanced things. With style."

"And the fog machines?"

"Let's just say too much rosemary oil in a small enclosed space has effects."

Selene sighed softly. "The mayor asked us not to participate in the contest that year."

"He begged," Elysse said.

Rowan glanced at the blinking scarecrow in the corner.

It was still blinking.

No one seemed to notice.

...Right," he said. "Keep it subtle."

Lyra leaned dramatically on the counter. "Alright. Story time."

Rowan glanced around like someone might save him.

No one did.

"So," Lyra began, "it was five years ago. Mayor Trent had just updated the town's fall event guide—made a big show about 'embracing the season' and 'tourism-driven charm.' We took that personally."

"We warned her," Elysse said, flipping through inventory cards like she didn't care. She absolutely cared.

"No you didn't," Lyra shot back. "You encouraged me."

"I told you not to use the haunted music box."

"Which," Talia added brightly, "sounded like children singing backwards."

Rowan froze. "That wasn't magical, right?"

"Mostly not," Lyra said. "I adjusted the tone just a little."

Selene, still calmly organizing fall-themed tea blends, chimed in. "You activated the haunting charm by accident."

"I tripped once."

"You tripped and screamed 'the spirits are loose.' In front of a tour group."

Lyra waved that off. "Anyway, we had enchanted candles that flickered when people lied—hilarious, by the way—and Talia built a scarecrow that followed people with its head."

"It was animatronic!" Talia defended. "And mostly safe!"

Rowan blinked. "Mostly?"

"And then," Lyra said with great satisfaction, "the mayor showed up."

Everyone went quiet for a second.

Rowan slowly set down the leaf garland. "What happened?"

Lyra grinned. "We don't talk about what happened."

Selene muttered, "The town had a curfew for three weeks."

"And a local priest got involved," Elysse added.

"It wasn't even real ectoplasm!" Talia protested.

"I don't care," Selene said. "We are not traumatizing more children this year."

Lyra winked. "No promises."

Lyra stretched, clearly satisfied with her retelling.

"Oh," she added casually, "and we got hit with a heavy fine."

Rowan blinked. "How heavy?"

"Twelve hundred dollars and a written apology to the town."

"Each?!"

"No, no—Selene paid it. She said it was worth it to make the mayor sweat."

Rowan stared at Selene like she'd just admitted to arson.

She didn't even blink. Just sipped her tea like it was justice.

"And Talia," Lyra continued, "had to do community service."

Talia gave a dramatic sigh. "Three weekends of trash pickup and pumpkin carving at the senior center. It was great."

"You made the elderly fight over who got to keep your jack-o'-lanterns," Elysse said without looking up.

"They were masterpieces," Talia said with a regal nod.

Rowan dropped his head into his hands. "Why am I living with you people."

Lyra reached over and patted his shoulder. "Because we're fun."

Selene stood.

"Enough talk," she said. "Decorations need finishing. Mayor Trent will be inspecting himself."

Rowan groaned.

Talia handed him a glittery cornucopia with absolutely no shame. And the fall chaos continued.

Chapter Twenty-Two — Quiet Before the Crowd

Summer in Ashford Landing didn't end in a blaze of glory. It faded gently, like the last breath of a lullaby. The breeze turned from heavy heat to a light caress, carrying the faint scent of dried leaves and cinnamon. Sunlight fell in long amber streaks across the pavement, and porch swings creaked softly in the hush between seasons.

Tourists, more and more each day, traded swimsuits and sunscreen for scarves and hot cider, and the Apothecary's window displays traded beach-themed potions for pumpkins and cinnamon-scented everything.

By the time the last box of decorations came up from the cellar, Rowan was convinced that Mayor Trent had somehow invented new shades of orange—specifically designed to offend the senses. There were felt pumpkins with obnoxiously cheery smiles, scarecrows wearing bowties, and garlands of autumn leaves that shimmered in the sunlight like an overly enthusiastic kindergarten craft project.

It was, in Rowan's private opinion, Halloween as designed for five-year-olds with absolutely no sense of humor.

"Is this level of orange really necessary?" Rowan asked, eyeing a particularly hideous wreath of foam pumpkins. "Like, legally?"

"Unfortunately, yes," Elysse said flatly, carefully placing decorative leaf-patterned candles on the shelves. "Ashford Landing code 23, subsection B. Autumn decorations must be 'inviting, seasonally appropriate, and non-threatening.'"

Rowan stared at her, incredulous. "Non-threatening? What would threatening autumn décor even look like?"

Elysse didn't look up. "Ask Lyra. She's still banned from judging the pumpkin carving contest."

"That was one time!" Lyra shouted from somewhere in the back. "They were creative!"

Rowan wisely chose not to ask for details. Instead, he quietly accepted his fate and taped a smiling paper squirrel wearing a tiny scarf to the window. He hoped sincerely that its innocent face would haunt Mayor Trent's dreams.

When the last glitter-covered scarecrow had been firmly positioned by the front door, Selene gave a satisfied nod and dismissed Rowan for lunch. Grateful to escape the overwhelming cheer, he grabbed his sketchpad, a sandwich wrapped neatly in parchment paper and fled to the solitude of the front stoop.

The stone beneath him was still sun-warmed, radiating a gentle heat through his jeans. A soft breeze stirred the loose pages of his sketchpad and carried the smell of roasted pecans from a vendor cart down the street. Somewhere, a wind chime sang lazily from a porch.

As he sank down onto the steps, sandwich in hand, Rowan exhaled slowly. It was peaceful here, with autumn sunlight filtering through the changing leaves and the distant hum of the town settling into its quieter season. He took a bite of his sandwich, savoring the calm—a rare moment where the world around him seemed content to slow down.

But of course, calm never lasted long in Ashford Landing.

Rowan leaned back against the worn wood, sketchpad propped comfortably on one knee, a half-eaten ham sandwich balanced precariously on the other. His shoulders still ached from training, a constant, quiet reminder that magic, despite its perks, came with plenty of bruises.

He took another bite of the sandwich, chewing slowly as he sketched absentmindedly, pencil drifting into loose, lazy shapes—curved lines and gentle shading, echoing the soft afternoon sunlight.

From inside the shop came the unmistakable voices of Lyra and Talia, locked in fierce debate.

"Candy corn is wax-coated lies!" Lyra declared with conviction. "It's like eating sadness."

Talia gasped theatrically. "That's candy blasphemy! It's tradition!"

"So were witch burnings. Traditions can be terrible."

"Did you just compare candy corn to witch trials?" Talia sounded both offended and amused. "Even for you, that's—"

"I stand by it," Lyra insisted, with an intensity that suggested she'd die defending this hill. "Candy corn is a scam forced upon innocent trick-or-treaters."

Rowan smiled faintly as he shaded a corner of the page. It didn't matter who won. The argument would inevitably resurface tomorrow—possibly about marshmallow pumpkins, which Lyra would also find morally offensive, and Talia would passionately defend.

For now, though, Rowan let their voices blend into background noise, just another comforting element of his daily life. Warm sunlight brushed against his skin, easing tired muscles and quieting the ache of exhaustion. These quiet moments—sandwich in hand, sketchbook open, the absurd soundtrack of his family debating candy in the background—were exactly what he needed.

He turned to a fresh page, beginning to carefully trace the curve of a nearby maple leaf, when a shadow fell across the sidewalk, darkening his paper.

"Excuse me?"

Rowan glanced up to see a woman standing uncertainly at the edge of the steps, clutching a colorful knit scarf around her neck despite the mild weather. She smiled hesitantly and pointed toward his sketchpad.

"Would you be willing to do a caricature for me?" she asked gently. Rowan quickly swallowed the last bite of his sandwich and nodded. "Sure." He picked up the sketchpad and started to draw.

The woman's face brightened with relief as she settled onto the small wooden stool Rowan kept beside him. Rowan picked up a fresh pencil, flipped to a clean page, and offered her a polite smile.

As he began sketching, the quiet rhythm of the afternoon returned. For now, things felt simple again—pencil lines, easy conversation, and the familiar comfort of an ordinary moment. At least, for now.

Rowan turned his sketchpad around, showing the finished caricature to the woman. She leaned forward eagerly, her smile broadening as she studied the exaggerated lines he'd carefully drawn.

She leaned forward with both hands pressed to her knees, laughter bubbling out before she could stop it. "Oh, it's wonderful!" she said, laughing gently as she examined the playful depiction of her colorful scarf, overly large smile, and kind eyes. "I love how cheerful you made me look."

Rowan smiled softly. "Well, you do look pretty cheerful."

"Thank you!" She reached into her pocket, pulling out a few crisp bills and placing them gently into his hand. "Keep the change. You did a great job."

Rowan murmured his thanks, quietly slipping the bills into his pocket. As she stepped away down the street, still smiling warmly at the drawing she'd tucked carefully under one arm, another voice rang out.

"Hey, are you still doing those?"

Rowan glanced up, blinking slightly in surprise as a man approached confidently, already moving to take the now-vacant seat. He wore a brand-new fleece vest embroidered with autumn leaves, clearly purchased from one of the tourist shops. He settled comfortably on the wooden stool, eyeing Rowan's sketchpad with obvious anticipation.

"Yeah," Rowan answered, quickly flipping to another blank page. "Just take a seat."

"Great," the man said, smiling broadly. "I figured a caricature would be a great way to remember this trip. You know, we're here for the authentic Halloween experience." He leaned in conspiratorially, like he was sharing a secret. "You locals really know how to embrace the season."

Rowan fought the urge to glance back at the shop's painfully sanitized decorations—felt pumpkins and smiling paper squirrels flashed briefly through his mind—and managed a polite smile instead. "I guess we do."

"Oh, definitely. My wife insisted on coming. Saw an article online, said this was the spot for a real old-school Halloween. Haunted shops, spooky inns, that kind of thing. Honestly, I'm just glad I found someone doing something genuinely local. I mean, how often do you see someone just sitting outside doing caricatures? It's perfect."

Rowan kept sketching, adding a comically oversized collar to the man's fleece vest. "Yeah, authenticity is...important."

The man continued enthusiastically, oblivious to Rowan's quiet amusement. "Absolutely. Halloween back home is just plastic decorations and candy aisles. Here, though? This feels real, you know?"

Rowan suppressed a laugh, glancing down at his drawing. "Definitely."

As he shaded the finishing touches on the tourist's caricature, Rowan quietly wondered what exactly counted as "authentic" in a town with a mayor who enforced mandatory scarecrow smiles.

Whatever it was, Rowan thought wryly, these tourists clearly loved it.

Rowan turned the sketchpad around again, showing the man his finished caricature. The tourist's eyes brightened immediately as he took in the exaggerated collar of his fleece vest, the overly enthusiastic grin Rowan had captured, and the slightly goofy tilt of his head.

"This is incredible!" the man laughed, reaching into his wallet without hesitation. "I can't wait to show my wife—she's gonna love it."

"Glad you like it," Rowan said politely, accepting the folded bills. "Enjoy the rest of your trip."

As the man stepped away, already admiring the drawing and grinning broadly, Rowan stretched his fingers slightly, preparing to close his sketchbook. Before he could even set down his pencil, however, another figure approached—this one a teenager wearing a sweatshirt emblazoned with the phrase "Ashford Landing: Where Halloween Lives."

"Hey, is this the caricature thing?" the teenager asked hopefully, glancing between Rowan and the small stool in front of him.

"Yeah," Rowan said, quickly masking his surprise. "You want one?"

"Totally!" the kid said, immediately plopping onto the stool and grinning broadly. "It looks way cooler than the pumpkin carvings down by the docks."

A breeze shifted through the square, rustling the leaves and the flyers pinned to the lamp posts. People began to glance over, pausing mid-step. A couple with iced cider cups slowed to watch. A child tugged her mother's sleeve and pointed. Before Rowan could close his sketchbook, the line had formed—quietly, casually, and entirely without his permission.

Rowan smiled despite himself, flipping to a fresh page and starting to sketch. As he worked, he noticed yet another pair of visitors standing a few feet away, whispering excitedly. By the time he'd finished the teenager's portrait—complete with a cartoonishly oversized sweatshirt and exaggeratedly spiked hair—a small but unmistakable line had formed along the sidewalk.

He stared at the growing crowd for a second, blinking slowly.

"Hey, uh, you're still open, right?" asked a young woman, clutching her purse and looking at him hopefully. "Your drawings are great— we'd really love one too."

Rowan hesitated just a second, glancing back toward the Apothecary. Inside, Talia and Lyra's debate over candy corn had seamlessly transitioned into an equally passionate argument about chocolate versus gummy candy.

Chapter Twenty-Three — Center of Attention

Rowan's pencil moved in looping arcs and sharp flicks, the graphite whispering over the page in bursts of motion. Smudges bloomed at the edge of his palm where he leaned too close, the paper warm beneath his fingers from the late-afternoon sun. He glanced up frequently, making small talk as he drew, doing his best to keep up with the faces and the increasingly impatient line in front of him.

But the line wasn't getting any shorter.

It was getting longer—faster than he could finish each drawing. Faces multiplied—muffled voices layered into a rising hum, the air thick with perfume, sunscreen, and the sugary scent of candied almonds from the vendor down the block. Every rustle of fabric or shifting footstep echoed too loud in his ears. A small crowd had formed now, some of them not even waiting for a turn— just standing nearby, openly staring as if he were some roadside attraction.

Rowan's shoulders tightened, tension creeping steadily down his back and into his hands. He had hoped for a quiet afternoon, maybe one or two sketches, a break from magic drills and debates over seasonal candy. But this was different. This was attention, curiosity, expectation, piling onto his shoulders with each new person who joined the line.

"Wow, how old is he?" whispered a woman nearby, craning her neck to watch. "Look at how fast he's drawing."

"Did you see that kid's caricature?" someone else murmured excitedly. "He's seriously good."

Rowan's face grew warm as he lowered his gaze, concentrating harder on the drawing in front of him. His pencil strokes became tighter, quicker—he could feel eyes pressing down on him, curious whispers prickling against his skin. He glanced up briefly and saw the line stretch even farther down the sidewalk, curling out past the Apothecary's window display.

Behind the glass, Talia paused mid-argument with Lyra, eyebrows lifting slightly as she caught sight of the growing crowd outside. Even she looked impressed, if a bit surprised.

Rowan swallowed hard, forcing himself to take a slow, steadying breath. It was fine. He could handle this. He just had to keep sketching.

But as he handed over another finished drawing—barely pausing before the next person eagerly took the vacated seat—Rowan couldn't help feeling a flicker of uncertainty deep in his stomach. He had never meant to be the center of anything—least of all attention.

Rowan pressed harder into the paper, pencil scratching swiftly across the surface, shading and outlining as quickly as his hand would allow. The crowd's murmuring had grown louder, anticipation building as people nudged forward, eager to watch his work.

The pencil cracked, splintering in his fingers like a twig underfoot. Graphite dust streaked across the paper. The sound, small but sharp, felt like a firecracker going off in his chest as he watched the tip roll onto the ground uselessly.

Rowan stared at it blankly, pulse jumping at the unexpected interruption. A small ripple of confusion moved through the crowd as he slowly stood up, rubbing his cramped fingers. "Uh, I'm gonna take a quick break," he murmured apologetically, stepping toward the Apothecary's front door. "Wait," said the woman next in line, sounding genuinely disappointed. "You're not done, are you?"
"No—no, I just need another pencil," Rowan said quietly, already uncomfortable as more eyes turned toward him.

People shifted closer, craning their necks curiously, some barely noticing they'd moved directly in front of the Apothecary's door. Rowan hesitated, feeling a sudden tightness in his chest. The line had spread, unintentionally blocking his path, the small crowd not even realizing they'd trapped him between the stoop and the shop.
"Excuse me," he murmured, voice barely audible over their chatter. "Can I just get—"

He shifted his weight forward, but his shoe caught on someone's bag. A shoulder brushed his arm. Laughter. A camera flash. The air thinned, his breath catching against the rising static under his skin. They didn't hear him, too busy talking and laughing among themselves, discussing drawings and taking pictures of the "caricature kid."

Rowan's throat tightened, anxiety surging quietly in his chest. It wasn't malicious—they weren't deliberately trapping him —but that didn't make him feel any less stuck. His fingers curled tighter around the broken pencil as he glanced toward the shop windows, hoping desperately for someone inside to notice his growing distress.

But through the glass, Talia and Lyra were busy ringing up customers, chatting cheerfully, completely unaware that Rowan had suddenly become trapped in his own unexpected popularity.

Rowan's heartbeat quickened, anxiety spiking sharply as the crowd pressed even closer, unaware they were blocking his path. His chest felt tight, breath shallow, the murmuring voices blending into a tense hum around him.

Without thinking, Rowan's voice broke out louder than he'd intended, strained with an edge of panic.

"Mom!"

The single word sliced through the noise, hanging awkwardly in the air for a moment.

Instantly, the Apothecary door swung open, and Selene stepped out, her calm eyes swiftly assessing the scene. Her quiet presence alone was enough to make people shuffle apart, creating a narrow but clear path.

"Come inside," she said gently, placing a reassuring hand on Rowan's shoulder. Her voice was steady, a soothing balm against his frayed nerves. "You're alright."

Rowan nodded wordlessly, breathing shakily as she guided him through the now-quiet crowd. Selene's presence was like an anchor, steady and sure, calming the tension that had wound so tightly in his chest.

As they crossed the threshold into the quiet sanctuary of the Apothecary, Selene turned slightly to close the door, ready to step back outside and disperse the waiting line.

But when she moved, she stopped abruptly.

Rowan didn't realize why at first. Then he felt it: his own fingers gripping the sleeve of her coat tightly, as if letting go meant falling back into uncertainty. His hand was trembling, white-knuckled, entirely beyond his control.

Selene turned back toward him, eyes softening instantly with gentle understanding.

"Rowan?" she said quietly, her voice barely above a whisper.

He looked up at her, eyes wide, uncertain, and vulnerable—but he didn't release her sleeve.

And in that moment, something shifted, soft and powerful, between them.

Rowan stood frozen, his fingers still locked tightly around the sleeve of Selene's coat, panic and embarrassment mingling uneasily in his chest. He waited for her to gently remove his hand, to quietly remind him that everything was fine. He waited for that calm, careful distance he'd grown used to his entire life.

Instead, Selene reached out quietly, and without a word, drew him into a soft embrace. Not tightly, but wholly; her coat smelled faintly of cloves and lavender.

It was a simple gesture—warm and effortless—but for Rowan, it felt strange, foreign. He stiffened instinctively at first, unused to the feeling, unused to anyone holding him like he mattered so effortlessly. But Selene didn't let go, her gentle arms around him steady, unwavering, patient.

Slowly, the rigid tension began to fade from his shoulders. He relaxed into the quiet certainty of her presence, the rhythm of her calm breathing, the comforting strength he hadn't realized he'd needed so desperately. It wasn't like any feeling he could easily name—it was strange, disarming, but above all, wonderfully safe.

When she finally pulled away, Rowan felt strangely lighter. His embarrassment was replaced by something softer, quieter, and much stronger.

"Better?" Selene asked softly, gently brushing a strand of hair from his forehead.

Rowan nodded, his throat too tight to trust his voice fully. "Yeah," he managed quietly, finally releasing her coat sleeve. "Thanks."

Selene gave a small, knowing smile, then turned calmly, reaching behind the counter for one of the shop's blank sketchbooks and a few bright-colored markers.

"What are you doing?" Rowan asked quietly, curious but still uncertain.

"Damage control," she answered simply, smiling softly. She opened the sketchbook with crisp precision, her pen gliding in deliberate strokes across the page. The scent of ink bloomed faintly in the air as she wrote: Caricatures: $25.

Rowan blinked in surprise, staring at the sign. "You—you're charging them now?"

"Of course," Selene replied easily, handing him the sign. "Your work has value, Rowan. You should never give it away for free."

Rowan took the sign, holding it lightly between his fingers, feeling the quiet certainty of Selene's words resonate deeply. She opened the door again, stepping outside to address the waiting crowd—calm, graceful, and entirely in control of the situation.

He watched her from the doorway, his chest strangely tight again, but for different reasons now. Because this was what it felt like, he realized, to have someone actually see him. To have someone care enough to hold him close, to steady him, and then quietly, carefully, set him back on his feet.

He glanced down at the sign in his hand, the letters neat and confident beneath his fingertips, and took a deep, steadying breath.

Then, quietly, he followed Selene back outside—ready to face the waiting crowd, knowing she would be right there behind him.

Chapter Twenty-Four —
Caricature Madness

The next few days passed in a whirlwind of pencil shavings, sketchpads, and seemingly endless faces. Rowan's little caricature stand, once just a quiet way to spend a lazy afternoon, had suddenly become the center of Ashford Landing's fall frenzy.

Each morning, he barely had time to finish his breakfast before a line began forming outside the Apothecary's door, tourists clutching coffee cups, chatting excitedly about "that kid who draws the funny pictures." The scent of cinnamon rolls drifted from the bakery next door as he hurried out, pencil already twitching in his fingers. By midday, the line would snake down the sidewalk, sometimes wrapping halfway around the block, eager faces patiently awaiting their turn.

His pencil moved faster and faster, each portrait flowing effortlessly from his fingertips onto the page. At first, he felt nervous—self-conscious about the way strangers would stare, pointing and murmuring. But gradually, he learned to tune out the whispered curiosity, finding instead a comforting rhythm within the steady, quick sketches.

Selene's carefully printed sign now proudly proclaimed his price—twenty-five dollars per caricature. Rowan still felt a little embarrassed whenever someone handed him the money, but he couldn't deny the satisfying weight of the bills in his pocket. He hadn't yet allowed himself to consider what he'd do with the money; for now, it simply felt good to have earned it.

Inside the Apothecary, Lyra and Talia found new amusement watching Rowan through the window, offering unsolicited commentary as the hours passed.

"He's drawing even faster today," Talia leaned against the warm wood of the front counter, cradling her coffee between ink-stained fingers, sipping coffee and leaning comfortably against the counter. "Think we should bring him a protein shake or something?"

"He's fine," Lyra replied, crouched by the display case, shifting a mischievously grinning pumpkin candle left by exactly one inch, then right again . "I survived the great pumpkin riot of five years ago; Rowan can handle caricature fever."

Elysse glanced at them both, a faint smile playing at the corner of her lips as she stacked freshly labeled soaps. "You're both enjoying this far too much."

"I don't know what you mean," Talia said innocently. "It's just nice seeing our Rowan blossom into Ashford Landing's newest tourist attraction."

Selene, quietly replenishing autumn-themed tea blends, allowed herself a small, amused sigh. "Let's not overwhelm him too quickly. He's still adjusting."

Outside, Rowan shaded in the oversized hat of yet another tourist, quietly marveling at how strange his life had become. His wrist ached with a dull, rhythmic throb, his fingertips blackened with graphite. Sweat prickled beneath his shirt despite the brisk air—part from the sun, part from nerves, and part from the strain of keeping his lines steady while his stomach grumbled. A few months ago, he'd been hiding behind dumpsters, digging through trash for scraps. Now, people willingly waited to pay him for drawings.

He lifted his gaze briefly, glancing at the steadily lengthening line, and couldn't quite suppress the small, bewildered smile that appeared on his face.

Caricature madness, he realized, wasn't so bad after all.

Rowan was busy shading in the wildly exaggerated sunglasses of a woman who kept laughing with delight each time she glanced down at her drawing. His fingers were aching from constant sketching, but it was a good kind of ache—earned, satisfying.

"Finished," he said quietly, handing over the caricature. "Hope you like it."

The woman beamed at him, eyes bright with excitement as she handed him a neatly folded stack of bills. "It's perfect! Thank you."

Rowan nodded politely, tucking the money into his pocket before glancing up to call the next customer forward. His smile froze abruptly as he saw who sat down.

It was a police officer, dressed casually in jeans and a fleece pullover, but the badge clipped to his belt was unmistakable. Beside him sat a young boy, probably no older than eight, bouncing excitedly and pointing at Rowan's sketchpad.

"Look, Dad! He's gonna draw us!" the kid said, grinning widely.

Rowan's heartbeat surged in his chest, and his fingers tightened instinctively around his pencil. He recognized the officer instantly—one of the cops who'd chased him down the back alleys of Ashford Landing a few months ago. He forced himself to breathe, willing his face to remain calm, but anxiety curled tightly in his stomach.

The officer studied Rowan carefully for a moment, his expression thoughtful, quietly assessing. Rowan swallowed nervously, pencil hovering uncertainly above the blank paper, dread pooling slowly inside him. He half expected the man to stand up, reach for his radio, and end the surreal normalcy he'd finally begun to trust.

Then, unexpectedly, the officer's serious expression softened into a gentle, reassuring smile. "It's okay," he said quietly. "Just a drawing for me and my son. That's all."

Rowan blinked, surprised, and felt some of the tension ease from his shoulders. He nodded cautiously, starting to sketch again, his pencil strokes uncertain at first but gradually steadying into their practiced rhythm.

The officer's young son watched with fascination, chatting happily. "Dad said you draw super fast! Can you make his ears look bigger? They're huge, right?"

The officer chuckled softly, nodding along. "Go ahead. He's right."

Rowan managed a small, hesitant smile, shading in the officer's exaggerated ears as carefully as he could. It felt strange—almost surreal—to be sitting so close to someone who'd once been a threat, now calmly allowing himself to be teased by his son.

When the drawing was finished, Rowan handed it over wordlessly, glancing up briefly to meet the officer's gaze. The man held Rowan's eyes for a brief moment, gentle but serious.

"You're good at this," the officer said softly, handing over a few bills. "Stay out of trouble, alright?"

Rowan nodded quietly, heart still thudding uneasily in his chest. "I'm trying."

The officer smiled again, patting his son on the shoulder as they stood up to leave. "You're doing just fine, kid. Keep it up."

As they walked away, Rowan watched them go, trying to shake off the lingering anxiety. But it was hard to ignore the quiet realization that had just sunk into his chest: He wasn't hiding anymore. He was visible now, recognizable. And that meant that old worlds and new worlds might keep colliding—whether he wanted them to or not.

When the line finally thinned enough for Rowan to take a short break, he gratefully set down his pencil and stretched his cramped fingers, grimacing slightly at the dull ache spreading through his wrist. He stood carefully, excusing himself to the waiting customers, and slipped inside the Apothecary.

He hadn't realized how hungry he was until the scent of takeout food hit him—rich, savory, and inviting. On the counter sat a neatly wrapped sandwich beside a carton of fries and a cup of ice-cold lemonade, condensation still beading down its sides. He stared at it for a moment, briefly confused, until he noticed the small handwritten note tucked beside the food.
Don't forget to eat. — Selene

Rowan smiled faintly, warmth spreading softly through his chest. Selene never made a fuss or drew attention to what she did. Instead, she quietly noticed the small things, anticipated his needs, and left her care behind in these gentle, thoughtful gestures. Rowan wondered if she even realized how much it meant to him—how each small kindness chipped slowly away at the walls he'd spent years building.

He grabbed the sandwich, savoring the quiet moment as he ate. With his other hand, he emptied his pockets of the neatly folded bills, carefully smoothing out each one before placing them into the small wooden box Selene had set aside for him behind the counter. It was nothing fancy—a simple cedar container, polished smooth by years of gentle use—but it felt like a treasure chest to Rowan, holding the tangible proof that he had earned something himself.

As he placed the money inside, he hesitated, fingertips brushing lightly over the stack of bills. He still wasn't sure what he would use it for, but the quiet pride he felt seeing it grow day by day was undeniable. It wasn't charity. It wasn't pity. It was his—earned honestly through skill, patience, and a determination he was still learning to trust in himself.

Finishing the sandwich and wiping his fingers clean, Rowan carefully closed the cedar box, letting his hand rest softly on its polished surface for a moment. He glanced toward the doorway, hearing the chatter and laughter of the line still waiting for him.

With a small smile, he reached for his sketchpad again and headed back outside, feeling lighter, steadier. Selene's quiet thoughtfulness had given him exactly what he needed, exactly when he needed it.

Back inside the Apothecary, Rowan took a quick moment to stretch, rolling his shoulders to loosen the stiffness that had settled into his muscles. He reached under the counter, finding the small bottle of herbal oil Selene had quietly left out for him, another one of her thoughtful, subtle gestures that seemed to anticipate his every need.

He poured a few drops onto his palms, carefully massaging it into his tired fingers, the gentle warmth soothing his aching joints almost immediately. The faint scent of lavender and mint drifted up, calming and reassuring, and he felt himself relax again, grateful for Selene's ever-present thoughtfulness.

Outside, the murmur of conversation had grown louder, and Rowan knew the crowd was waiting patiently for him. He took a deep breath, giving his hands one final stretch before quickly stepping back into the bright autumn sunlight. The line had swelled once more, tourists chatting excitedly as they spotted him returning.

"Sorry about that," Rowan called out apologetically, sliding into his seat and flipping open his sketchpad with renewed determination. "Who's next?"

"That would be me," answered a smooth, familiar voice.

The sidewalk noise seemed to dip, voices dimming around the edges. Rowan looked up—and felt the cold weight of familiarity coil low in his stomach before he even recognized the voice. Lucian sat calmly, a faint, knowing smile on his lips.

"Hello again, Rowan."

Chapter Twenty-Five — The Offer

Rowan's initial surprise quickly faded, replaced instead by a slow-building sense of defiance. Lucian might have surprised him, yes—but Rowan refused to let him see even a hint of uncertainty. He squared his shoulders, calmly met Lucian's gaze, and lifted his pencil with quiet confidence.

"Hold still," Rowan said mildly, flipping to a fresh page and raising his eyebrows in exaggerated appraisal. He adjusted his grip on the pencil, feeling the familiar weight settle into his hand like armor. The sounds of the street—laughter, rustling leaves, the scrape of boots—faded to background static as he focused. "Caricatures need personality. I'll have to work extra hard with you."

Lucian's mouth twitched in amused acknowledgment, leaning back comfortably. "Take your time. I'm in no rush."

Rowan smirked faintly, pencil gliding confidently across the paper. He knew he should be afraid—Lucian had power, influence, and something dangerous simmering beneath that carefully polished surface—but at this moment, Rowan felt strangely calm. Maybe it was the warmth of Selene's subtle care lingering in his hands, or the absurdity of Lucian Aubrey sitting patiently on a stool, like every other tourist he'd drawn today. Whatever it was, Rowan let it fuel his quiet defiance.

Lucian studied Rowan carefully, silent for several seconds, allowing the quiet chatter of the waiting crowd to fill the gap. Finally, he spoke, voice quiet and calm—almost pleasant. "You seem quite content here," Lucian observed. "It's charming, really. All of this simplicity."

Rowan lifted an eyebrow, shading in the careful angles of Lucian's collar. "It's a good life. Quiet, honest. You should try it sometime."

Lucian chuckled softly, utterly unbothered by Rowan's gentle jab. "Perhaps. But I think you know as well as I do that simplicity rarely lasts. Eventually, reality comes knocking."

Rowan shrugged lightly, adding a deliberately exaggerated arch to Lucian's perfectly groomed eyebrows. "Reality knocked already. Turns out I'm pretty good at caricatures."

Lucian's smile widened fractionally, his gaze steady, calculating. "Of course. But surely you know there's more. Much more."

Rowan continued sketching, quietly defiant, determined to show Lucian he wasn't rattled. "If you say so."

"Oh, I do," Lucian replied, voice smooth, soft, and absolutely certain. "And I'm here to tell you what Selene won't."

Rowan glanced up, meeting Lucian's cool gaze directly, his heart giving one small, traitorous flutter of uncertainty before he steadied himself again.

"Alright then," Rowan said mildly, pencil poised confidently above the page. "Let's hear your big secret."

Lucian leaned forward slightly, his smile unwavering, though the warmth in it never quite reached his eyes.

"You're clever," Lucian said softly a gust of wind stirred fallen leaves across the sidewalk, brushing against Rowan's boots like something whispering just out of reach. He didn't flinch, but the cold bit through his jacket all the same. "I'll grant you that. You've clearly learned how to survive. But I wonder—do you realize that's all you've been doing?"

Rowan's pencil slowed, his confident expression faltering slightly despite his best efforts. Lucian's voice was gentle, but his words had a sharpness beneath them, carefully cutting through Rowan's newfound security.

Lucian continued calmly, almost conversationally, "Selene has given you a comfortable illusion, Rowan. But she's only shown you the surface. The quaint shop, the thoughtful gestures—yes, it's charming. But she hasn't given you the truth."

Rowan's stomach tightened quietly, dread curling slowly through him as Lucian held his gaze, effortlessly in control.

"You're powerful. More powerful than she dares to admit to you—or perhaps even herself," Lucian said, eyes steady and intent. "Your lightning alone marks you as special. Rare. Dangerous, even. You've seen glimpses of what you're capable of—but imagine what you could do if you weren't held back by sentiment and caution."

Rowan forced himself to speak, voice tight. "You mean like you?"

Lucian smiled faintly, utterly unfazed. "Exactly like me. You see, I've embraced what I am. I don't pretend otherwise. But you—" Lucian shook his head lightly, disappointed. "You allow Selene to limit you. To keep you comfortably small. To make you... manageable."

Rowan's heart thudded uncomfortably against his ribs, Lucian's words slicing precisely into the doubts he'd quietly buried. The truth was, he had felt it—Selene's careful caution, the gentle warnings hidden behind every lesson. And suddenly, he wasn't certain if she'd been protecting him...or protecting everyone else from him. He kept drawing, but the pencil tip trembled faintly with each stroke, smudging the corner of Lucian's throat.

Lucian leaned back, satisfied by Rowan's wavering expression. "You're settling for crumbs, Rowan, when you could have everything. Power. Freedom. The truth. All you need to do is step beyond the comfort of Selene's careful lies."

Rowan stared down at his half-finished drawing, fingers tight around his pencil, heart hammering quietly in his chest.

"Think carefully," Lucian murmured softly. "Ask yourself: has Selene really given you answers, or just another cage?"

Rowan stared quietly at the drawing in front of him, his pencil poised but motionless. Lucian's words lingered like echoes in his mind, heavy and unsettling. He knew it was manipulation, knew Lucian was weaving truths and half-truths expertly together, yet he couldn't deny the small, insidious seed of doubt that had taken root deep inside him.

Still, Rowan lifted his head slowly, meeting Lucian's calm, patient gaze.

"I appreciate your concern," Rowan said softly, voice steady despite the uneasy twist in his chest. "But I trust Selene."

Lucian's eyes narrowed slightly, the barest flicker of disappointment crossing his composed features. "Even if she's holding you back?"

Rowan forced himself to smile, calmness masking the quiet unease beneath. "If this is being held back, I'm okay with it."

Lucian tilted his head slightly, studying Rowan carefully. A quiet tension stretched between them before Lucian let out a gentle sigh, feigning regret. "And you're truly content, then? Sketching silly cartoons for strangers who pay to be entertained by a curiosity—a dancing monkey with a pencil?"

Rowan's jaw tightened slightly, pencil moving again, sketching Lucian's features with quick, precise strokes, deliberately exaggerating his carefully cultivated arrogance.

"Better a dancing monkey than a puppet," Rowan replied mildly, shading Lucian's expression with exaggerated disdain. "Maybe you're just jealous that people actually like what I do." He pressed harder with the pencil, darkening the lines around Lucian's eyes, exaggerating the smug tilt of his chin. His smirk was dry but steady.

Lucian's eyes flashed briefly—irritation, perhaps—but he quickly smoothed his expression, once again unreadable.

"Jealousy isn't becoming," Lucian murmured softly, a faint smile returning. "And pride can blind as surely as ignorance. Remember that."

Rowan didn't respond, shading the caricature quietly, his defiance unwavering, even as Lucian's subtle warnings whispered softly at the edges of his thoughts.

The truth was, Lucian's words had touched something vulnerable inside him. Rowan did wonder—just for a moment—if he was settling for less, if there were truths Selene had quietly withheld, if perhaps Lucian's promises held even the smallest kernel of truth. But the moment passed quickly, buried beneath Rowan's fierce determination not to show Lucian weakness again.

He tore the finished drawing carefully from the pad, and with quiet, deliberate confidence, handed Lucian the paper.

Lucian accepted the caricature with a quiet, amused smile, carefully examining Rowan's intentionally unflattering depiction of his cool arrogance. Without comment, he stood smoothly, adjusting his immaculate coat, eyes briefly glancing down at Rowan with a subtle, unreadable expression.

"Consider our conversation carefully, Rowan," Lucian murmured, slipping a hand casually into his pocket. "When you tire of being a sideshow, remember that I offered you a chance at more."

He placed something down on the small wooden stool and turned away, blending effortlessly into the passing crowd. Rowan stared after him, heart still hammering quietly in his chest, until Selene's voice broke gently through his uneasy thoughts.

"Rowan?" she called softly, stepping outside onto the stoop, eyes narrowed with quiet concern. "Is everything alright? I thought I saw—"

She stopped abruptly, noticing Rowan's tense expression and the empty stool.

Rowan forced himself to smile lightly, attempting to disguise the lingering unease in his chest. "I'm fine. Lucian was just here."

Selene's expression sharpened immediately, stepping closer and gently resting a reassuring hand on his shoulder. "Did he hurt you?"

"No," Rowan said quietly, shaking his head, voice calmer now. "Just talked. Nothing new, really."

He glanced down at the stool, noticing the crisp hundred-dollar bill Lucian had left behind—a silent reminder, a subtle taunt. Rowan reached down, taking the money into his fingers and staring at it silently for a moment, considering its meaning.

Then, quietly and deliberately, he crumpled it in his fist, stood, and walked directly to the trash bin beside the Apothecary's door. Without hesitation, he tossed the bill inside, turning back to Selene with a determined glint in his eyes.

Selene watched silently, something like quiet pride flickering in her expression. "What was that?"

Rowan shrugged gently, though his voice carried quiet conviction. "Lucian paid extra for the drawing," he said lightly. "But I think his money is worth even less than his promises."

A faint smile touched Selene's lips as she squeezed Rowan's shoulder gently. "Good."

Rowan felt warmth spread quietly through his chest, the unease fading slowly into a determined calm. He was shaken, yes—Lucian's words still lingered quietly—but here, beside Selene, it felt manageable again.

"Come inside," she said softly, guiding him gently toward the Apothecary's door. "You deserve a break."

He nodded gratefully, glancing once more toward the crowded street, half expecting Lucian to reappear.

But the sidewalk was clear now, empty except for tourists, laughter, and bright autumn sunlight. The only shadow Lucian left behind was the crumpled bill in the trash, a quiet, discarded promise.

Chapter Twenty-Six — Birthday Math

Late-afternoon sunlight slanted through the apothecary's front windows, catching on the curls of steam rising from Talia's drink and throwing warm amber across the polished floorboards. Rowan was once again crouched behind the counter, tucking another wad of cash into the small cedar box Selene had set aside for him. The bills were neatly folded, organized by denomination, and growing steadily in size—enough now that the lid no longer closed flush without a bit of coaxing. He shoved it closed with the side of his fist and gave it a satisfying thunk.

"You're going to need a bank account," Talia said from her perch on a nearby stool, sipping something iced and aggressively sweet. She was watching him with an expression halfway between impressed and exasperated. "Seriously. That box is starting to look like it belongs to a raccoon with a gambling addiction."

Rowan shrugged, grabbing another handful of bills from his pockets. "It works."

"For now," Talia said, spinning slightly on the stool. "But if you keep pulling in cash like this, you're going to have to start paying taxes."

Rowan froze, a single bill still pinched between his fingers like it had suddenly turned venomous. A cold sweat prickled the back of his neck. "T-Taxes? I'm twelve!"

Talia's grin widened instantly. "Oh yeah. Income, self-employment, local, state—gotta fund the town's glitter scarecrow program somehow."

Rowan gave her a look of abject horror, then slowly turned his attention back to the cedar box like it had just betrayed him. "I didn't agree to any of that."

"Welcome to capitalism," Talia said cheerfully. "Now you're not just a contributing member of society—you're a target."

"I take it back," Rowan muttered. "No more drawings. Everyone gets stick figures."

From across the room, Lyra let out a snort. "You wouldn't last three hours. You live for the drama of making someone's nose huge."

"Yeah, but they don't tax noses," Rowan grumbled.

Talia leaned forward with mock seriousness. "Not yet."

Elysse, perched beside the herb-drying rack and surrounded by tiny glass bottles, continued labeling tinctures with the steady precision of someone timing a spell. She didn't even look up. "Actually, he can't open a bank account. He's not fourteen."

Rowan blinked. "Seriously?"

"Seriously," Elysse replied calmly. "Fourteen is usually the minimum for opening a custodial account, and even then, you'd need identification, proof of address, a guardian to sign, and possibly a blood sample depending on the bank."

Rowan looked down at his money box like it was radioactive. "So, what am I supposed to do? Bury it in the yard?"

"Technically," Elysse continued, now turning toward the counter with one brow slightly raised, "you shouldn't even be working for us without parental consent or legal documentation."

Talia gasped dramatically, spinning back toward him. "You're an outlaw."

"I am not."

"You are. A little art bandit with a sandwich addiction."

Rowan rolled his eyes, but a smile tugged at the corner of his mouth. "I'm not an outlaw. I'm just not...documented."

"Uh-huh." Talia leaned on the counter. "So when do you turn fourteen?"

Rowan didn't even look up from folding another bill. "Fifty-four weeks."

There was a beat of silence. And then, very slowly, every head in the room turned.

Lyra squinted. "Wait. Fifty-four weeks?"

Elysse raised a brow, amused.

Talia dropped her drink. "Oh no," Rowan said, realizing too late what he'd done.

Lyra spun around, eyes narrowing like she'd just spotted a puzzle on the verge of solving itself. "You said fifty-four weeks?"

Rowan hesitated, visibly calculating the odds of making it to the back door before anyone could do anything about it. Not good.

"Fifty-four is an oddly specific number," Lyra continued, already pacing. "Fifty-two weeks in a year, so your birthday's in—"

"Thirteen months," Talia said, sliding in beside her like a detective on a crime show. "No—wait. That's not right. Fifty-four minus fifty-two..."

"Two weeks," Elysse supplied helpfully from across the room. "His birthday's in two weeks."

Lyra turned slowly, eyes locked on Rowan. "Is your birthday in two weeks, Rowan?"

"No."

"Liar," she said immediately, pointing at him.

"You hesitated."

"I didn't hesitate."

"You blinked weird," Talia added. "That's a guilty blink. Classic rookie mistake."

"I blinked like a normal person!"

Lyra snapped her fingers dramatically. "Get the calendar."

Rowan stood up, backing toward the shelves. "Okay, everybody calm down—"

"Oh, we're calm," Talia said, now actively rummaging through drawers. "We're just determined."

"This is why I didn't tell you," Rowan muttered under his breath.

Lyra leaned over the counter, grinning. "It's within two weeks, isn't it?"

Rowan crossed his arms. "I'm not saying anything."

"Is it tomorrow?" Talia asked.

"No."

"Is it the next day?"

"No."

"Full moon?" Lyra offered.

"No."

"Is it Halloween?" Talia said, half-joking, half-serious.

Rowan went very still.

Lyra's grin grew wicked. "Oh. Ohhhhh."

Talia gasped and nearly dropped her drink a second time. "No way. Are you serious?"

Rowan sighed, resigning himself to fate. "Yes. Okay? It's Halloween."

The room went still. Even the kettle on the back burner seemed to stop mid-bubble, as if the apothecary itself had heard and gasped. Then the room exploded.

"What do you mean it's Halloween?" Talia shouted, hands flying into her hair. "That's the busiest day of the year!"

"Which is exactly why I didn't say anything," Rowan muttered, sinking lower into his chair like he could disappear through the floorboards.

Lyra paced in a tight circle, muttering to herself. "No, no, no. This is a sacred day. Halloween is peak chaos energy. We can't let this go unobserved."

"It's fine," Rowan said quickly, waving his hands. "Really. I don't even care about my birthday."

"You shut your beautiful, under-celebrated face," Talia snapped, pointing dramatically. "This changes everything."

"We could do breakfast," Elysse offered helpfully, already flipping through the planner they kept under the counter. "We open late on Halloween so we can prep the shop. If we shift candle rotations to the night before…"

"No," Rowan groaned, covering his face. "I'm begging you—please don't rearrange the schedule for me."

"I will rearrange the universe for you," Talia declared, tossing a tea strainer over her shoulder like it was a war banner. "You think Halloween is busy now? Wait till you're trying to sell soap while we also celebrate your BIRTH."

Lyra pointed toward the ceiling like she was invoking some ancient law. "You can't not celebrate a Halloween birthday. That's not a thing."

"I think it is a thing," Rowan muttered.

"Not in this house it isn't!" Talia yelled.

Elysse didn't even look up. "We'll keep it simple. Just a special breakfast, maybe a small present. We'll keep it subtle so it doesn't overwhelm him."

"I'm right here!" Rowan said as his ears started to turn pink. Talia and Lyra both ignored him and turned toward Elysse, scandalized.

"You call breakfast a birthday?" Talia asked.

"We are witches," Lyra said. "We summon storms. We brew chaos. We do not do subtle."

"I hate all of this," Rowan said, already regretting everything.

"Too late," Lyra called, already heading for the stairs. "Operation Spook cake is officially underway!"

"Wait, what is—"

"Don't worry about it," Talia said, clapping him on the back. "Just show up. And don't eat anything suspicious-looking."

Rowan buried his face in his arms as they scattered like confetti in a windstorm, their footsteps creaking across the wood floor and echoing up the stairs. "I should've just paid the taxes," he muttered.

Chapter Twenty-Seven — Paperwork

The last customer stepped out into the autumn air with a cheerful thank you, the little bell above the door jingling its farewell as it swung shut. The silence that followed was immediate and sacred.

Talia groaned and dropped into one of the display chairs near the window, dramatically flinging her arm over her eyes. "We survived," she announced. "Barely."

"I think that woman tried to haggle with me using coupons from 2007," Lyra muttered, flipping the "CLOSED" sign in the window before locking the door. "And she wasn't even sure what she wanted. She said, and I quote, 'Something that smells purple.'"

Elysse was already sweeping behind the counter, entirely unfazed. "Lavender and blackcurrant. I gave her a seasonal bundle."

"Of course you did," Talia mumbled.

Rowan was quiet as he knelt behind the counter, prying open the wooden box he kept tucked away under the till. His fingers fumbled as he tried, for the third time today, to shove another folded wad of bills inside. The box lid refused to close. Again. He sighed and sat back on his heels, watching as the top popped back open like it was judging him.

"Problem?" Elysse asked, without looking up.

"My box is full."

There was a beat of silence. Talia slowly sat up, suddenly interested. "How full are we talking?"

Rowan held up the cedar box—stuffed, bent, and bulging with rolled cash. It looked less like a savings container and more like a magician's hat that had lost a bet.

"Oh," Lyra said, eyes narrowing. "That's real full."

"Which brings us to a legal dilemma," Elysse said casually, like she'd been waiting for this. "We may want to look into something official soon. Tax stuff, guardianship, inheritance, health records..."

Rowan raised an eyebrow. "Health records?"

"You'll thank me when you need a dentist," she replied.

Lyra leaned on the counter. "What's the easiest way to do all that?"

Elysse paused, then looked over at Rowan. "Formal adoption."

Everything went still; Rowan's heartbeat tripped, a flutter behind his ribs like he'd missed a step on the stairs or been reminded of something he'd forgotten.

There was a silence—a real one this time, heavy and sudden. Talia blinked like she hadn't heard Elysse correctly. Lyra straightened, her grin gone, brows lifting with something that looked suspiciously like surprise. Rowan sat very still, the cash box still balanced in his lap.

"Oh," Talia said at last, her voice noticeably quieter. "You mean like... official-official."

Elysse nodded, tone still matter-of-fact. "It's the cleanest legal route. Covers school, medical, taxes, employment. Makes everything easier in the long run."

Rowan's hands tightened slightly around the edges of the box. "We're just floating the idea," Elysse added gently. "It's not something we'd spring without—"

"Obviously I should be the one to do it," Talia said, suddenly back in motion and waving one arm grandly. "I've spent the most time shaping his cultural identity. I introduced him to sesame chicken. I got him to eat a vegetable. That's, like, foundational parenting."

Lyra scoffed. "Please. I took him to a steakhouse and tripled his worldview. I win."

"You let him eat cake for dinner."

"It was a bonding experience."

As they bickered, Rowan's eyes flicked toward Selene, standing quietly near the shelves, her hands still dusted with dried lavender from the sachet jars she'd been refilling. She wasn't saying anything. Rowan's heart thudded once in his chest.

He knew they were joking—of course they were. This was how the Aubreys operated: chaos first, logic second. But somewhere beneath all the noise, a familiar fear stirred. What if she doesn't want to? What if this was one of those moments where everyone laughed and made a joke, and when the dust settled, someone kindly explained that some people just weren't meant to be permanent?

Rowan kept his eyes on Selene, trying not to let the worry show, but he could feel it tightening across his chest like a knot pulled too tight.

Then—wordlessly—Selene looked over and smiled. Not a forced smile. Not one of polite reassurance. A real, quiet, gentle smile that reached her eyes and said everything she didn't need to say.

Rowan exhaled, his grip on the box easing.

Immediately, both Lyra and Talia noticed the exchange.

Lyra groaned and threw her arms up in theatrical defeat. "Oh come on, you're just going to give it to her?"

"She didn't even campaign!" Talia added, pointing an accusing finger. "I had a whole speech ready."

Selene tilted her head slightly, still smiling. "I didn't realize this was a competition."

"That's exactly what someone who's winning would say," Lyra muttered.

"I demand joint custody," Talia said, half to me, half to the store.

"Absolutely not," Lyra replied. "He's already seen you trying to eat glitter."

Rowan snorted, shoulders relaxing for the first time in minutes.

"I'll get the paperwork started after the holiday," Elysse said calmly, as if none of the chaos were happening around her. "No rush, but the sooner we start the better."

Rowan nodded slowly, still holding the overstuffed cedar box. Something had changed in the room—something warm and steady that settled in his chest like the moment after the fall, when you realize someone actually caught you.

He glanced back toward Selene, and for once, didn't look away.

As the room shifted back to normal—Lyra and Talia returning to their good-natured squabbling, Elysse calmly organizing paperwork as if none of it fazed her—Rowan lingered near Selene, the box still in his hands. She noticed.

"What's on your mind?" she asked softly, her tone light, but not dismissive.

Rowan hesitated, then held out the cedar box like it weighed a hundred pounds. "I want to help pay for it. The adoption."His hands trembled slightly—not from fear, but from the sheer vulnerability of asking to matter this much.

Selene blinked, a little surprised. "Rowan—"

"I need this." he interrupted gently. "I need to feel like I helped."

There was a pause—just long enough for Rowan to think he'd said something wrong.

Then Selene smiled. Not the quiet smile from before—this one was proud, and warm, and just a little relieved around the edges.

"Okay," she said, placing her hand over the box but not taking it. "Then we'll do it together."

Rowan nodded, swallowing around something tight in his throat. "How much is it gonna cost?" he asked, trying to keep his voice light.

Talia wandered over just in time to hear. "Yeah, let's see how much damage you're doing."

Rowan opened the box and said, "About two thousand."

Talia whistled low. "Okay, moneybags. Look at you."

Lyra leaned in from across the room, eyes wide. "You've been holding out on us."

Then Elysse, perfectly deadpan: "Average adoption runs around thirty grand."

Rowan stared.

Talia let out a low whistle.

"Does that include snacks?" Lyra asked. "Because he might be able to cover the snacks."

Selene chuckled softly beside him. "Don't worry," she said. "You've already done the hard part."

Rowan looked up at her. "What's that?"

"Deciding if you want to stay."

Rowan's face felt hot, he nodded quiet and steady as he felt the warmth of her words settle into his chest.

Chapter Twenty-Eight — The Blur

The days that followed were a blur, Rowan couldn't remember the last time the Apothecary was quiet. The century old building swelled with customers from open to close, the storefront practically vibrating with the scent of cinnamon brooms, cedarwood candles, and too many people asking if "witches really lived here.". All the while cedarwood candles bleed warmth into the windowsills and clove infused soaps perfumed the air until it felt like you could chew it. Rowan worked through it all—hauling boxes, stacking shelves, bagging purchases, and occasionally disappearing behind the counter to shove more money into the second cedar box Selene had set up for him when the first one officially gave up.

Outside, the leaves burned bright orange and red before tumbling into damp, rustling heaps. Wind pulled at the fake cobwebs strung between windows, tugging them loose until they fluttered like old ghosts. A few had tangled in the lampposts, catching bits of falling leaves like forgotten decorations.

Tourists snapped selfies in front of scarecrows and plastic jack-o'-lanterns while Rowan silently judged every lopsided display with the eye of someone who had stacked too many fall-themed soap pyramids for it to be funny anymore.

Inside the shop, the atmosphere was pure controlled chaos. Talia's "seasonal display cauldron" overflowed hourly with glittery potion bottles and pumpkin-shaped soap. Lyra was running tarot readings like a street performer with flair, flair, and more flair, and Elysse seemed to have become the resident customer traffic coordinator—part librarian, part traffic cop.

By the end of each shift, his shoulders ached like they'd been packed in soap crates, and the skin of his fingers felt raw from twine and price tags. He didn't have the energy to complain—just enough to breathe and keep moving. There was no time to overthink, to worry, or to get in his own head about things like paperwork or birthdays or... what it meant to be wanted. He just moved through the blur, one customer at a time.

Until it stopped.

Until the morning came bright and crisp, with low-hanging fog on the edges of the road and the faintest scent of woodsmoke in the air. It was Halloween. His birthday.

Rowan came downstairs expecting to be handed a broom, a box of candles, or a list of things to restock. Instead, Selene was already waiting by the door with her coat on and a travel mug of coffee in each hand.

"Put your shoes on," she said. "We're heading into town."

Rowan blinked at her. "Shouldn't we be, I don't know... elbow-deep in pumpkin soap by now?"

"I sent Talia and Lyra to the shop early," she said, handing him one of the mugs. "They can handle the chaos."

"That feels like a bold claim."

"They're supervised."

"By who?"

"Elysse."

"Oh. Okay then."

He took a sip, eyes narrowing as the familiar taste hit him. Not just coffee—his coffee. The way he liked it. She'd remembered.

They walked down into town together, the streets already buzzing with tourists dressed in cozy flannels and felt witch hats, some pulling their kids along in wagons filled with pumpkins or toddlers in costume. The air smelled like chimney smoke, cider, and sugar—the kind that clung to the corners of your clothes long after you'd gone home.

Selene didn't say where they were going. She didn't have to. The costume shop stood near the end of the street, decked out in gaudy orange banners and black lace curtains. A plastic bat flapped above the door as they stepped inside.

The air smelled like rubber masks and dry glitter. One aisle screamed with neon feather boas, another shimmered with fairy wings that blinked when you passed. Rowan hesitated at the entrance, blinking like he'd just stepped onto another planet.

Selene leaned in and said, perfectly casual, "Might as well look around while we're here."

Rowan looked at her. She looked at the fake vampire teeth. They both knew what this was.

He sighed, already resigned to the outcome. "You're not subtle."

"I didn't try to be."

After a few laps around the shop pretending he wasn't interested, Rowan finally stopped in front of a costume on the far wall. It wasn't flashy or glittery or stitched with fake muscles—it was simple: a tunic with ornate piping, a short cloak, a pair of soft boots, and a little hat with a feather tucked in one side. The tag read: Pied Piper.

Selene raised an eyebrow. "Interesting choice."

Rowan shrugged. "I like the colors."

She didn't push. Just nodded and took it up to the counter without another word, paying in cash and handing him the bag with the kind of grace that made it feel like a gift even though he knew it wasn't.

They walked back together in companionable silence, Rowan fiddling with the feather in the cap as they cut through side streets. By the time they returned to the shop, the sidewalk outside was already overflowing with people—some in costumes, some in matching "Ashford Landing Authentic Halloween Experience" shirts.

The Apothecary had been transformed. The air inside was dense with clove, cedar, and something sweet Rowan couldn't name. Candles flickered in every window, glowing orange and gold while casting shifting shadows over bundled herbs and curling smoke. The dried herbs hung like garlands from the awning. The scent of clove and cedar hung thick in the air. A black chalkboard sat near the entrance, boasting "Witch-Approved Remedies for the Modern Mortal!" in swirling white script.

Inside the shop stood four women—Elysse at the counter, Talia near the potions display, Lyra perched dramatically on the staircase railing, and Selene already hanging her coat on the wall. All of them were dressed in long black gowns, white collars, and high-necked sleeves. Their hair was pinned up or tucked under modest bonnets.

They looked like something out of a Salem courtroom.

Rowan blinked.

Elysse looked up over her spectacles. "We're reclaiming the aesthetic."

Talia spun dramatically, her skirts flaring. "Honestly? I look amazing."

"We all do," Lyra said, lifting her chin. "Terrifying, repressed, and extremely fashionable."

"Let me guess," Rowan said dryly, setting down the costume bag. "You planned this just to mess with tourists."

Selene gave a small, satisfied nod. "Of course."

Outside, the town's Halloween festivities had officially begun. Laughter and chatter spilled in through the open windows, children darted past in a blur of capes and plastic pumpkins, and the line forming outside the Apothecary was already bending around the corner.

By the time the sun slipped behind the hills and the sky turned lavender with the promise of night, Ashford Landing was alive with music, lights, and the scent of sugar and smoke.

The Apothecary pulsed with activity—visitors weaving in and out in a steady stream, cameras flashing, children pressing their noses to the glass displays. Rowan sat cross legged near the front window dressed in his Pied Piper costume and sketching between waves of customers. A few kids had stopped just to stare at him—half enchanted, half unsure if he was part of the event or just someone very committed to the bit as he handed them candy and small tokens.

He didn't mind. There was something nice about just existing in the middle of it all—floating through the noise without being the center of it.

Which, as it turned out, would not last.

Because Lyra had other plans.

The lights in the Apothecary flickered once—intentional, dramatic. Then Lyra emerged from the back, slowly, carefully holding a cake. A real cake. Thirteen candles flickered on top, casting an amber glow over her smug, delighted expression.

She stepped onto the front stoop like it was a stage, cleared her throat with theatrical flair, and announced:

"Attention, Ashford Landing!"

Half the tourists turned. Some clapped instinctively. One person dropped a caramel apple.

Lyra raised the cake high. "We are gathered here tonight to celebrate the birth of this majestic little gremlin—Rowan—who is now officially thirteen years old."

There was a stunned beat of silence.

Then Talia burst through the door, arms wide. "He's legal enough to work but not enough to drive!"

"And arguably more emotionally stable than all of us!" Elysse added, deadpan from inside.

Rowan just froze—somewhere between horror and disbelief—mouth open, eyes wide.

And then Lyra started singing. Loudly.

The crowd joined in. Happy Birthday echoed up and down the street, blending with the music and laughter of the night. Tourists

who didn't even know him clapped along. Someone with a
tambourine tried to add percussion. The girl dressed as a bat
standing near the cider booth teared up halfway through the song
and whispered, "That's so cute."
Rowan stood in the doorway, face flushed, ears red, caught
between mortified and—if he was honest—kind of touched.
Lyra handed him the cake as the final "to youuuu" trailed off into
cheers.
"Blow 'em out, Birthday Boy," she said smugly.
Rowan stared at the candles, then at her, then at the crowd.
And laughed. Quietly, helplessly, a real laugh.
Then he blew out the candles.

Chapter Twenty-Nine — The Shift

By morning, Halloween was already a memory. The jack-o'-lanterns that had lit the streets just hours earlier sat cold and sagging on porch steps, their grins melting inward. Shop windows that had been frosted with cobwebs and flickering candles were suddenly scrubbed clean. The scarecrows were gone. The fake blood hosed off the sidewalks. And someone—probably Trent, the mayor, because of course it was—had already swapped the town square banners from orange and black to deep reds and glitter-drenched gold.

Ashford Landing didn't take its time easing into the next season: it leapt. The scent of scorched pumpkin still lingered faintly in the gutters, trampled candy wrappers stuck to the soles of tourists' boots, but above them, the town was already gleaming with fake frost and cinnamon air freshener.

By noon, wreaths were going up. By three, someone had started stringing lights between the lampposts. The bookstore down the street had swapped its window display from ghost stories and gothic romances to snow-dusted novels and a cardboard cutout of Santa holding a copy of A Christmas Carol.

Rowan stood outside the Apothecary with a broom in hand, the brittle leaves crumbled under the bristles, snapping like dry paper as he swept. A gust of wind caught one and sent it tumbling into the gutter, where it vanished beneath a pair of glitter-covered snow boots.

Halloween had barely left the stage before Christmas pushed past it in full costume. The world had already spun past his birthday, like a carousel too fast to hold onto. He stood still while everything around him blurred into garlands and LED lights. He wasn't sure how he felt about that yet.

The cider barrels were gone.

The paper bats had vanished.

And the chalkboard out front had been wiped clean.

It was November.

Rowan sighed, brushing a few leaves off his sleeve. "That was fast."

Behind him, Lyra stuck her head out the door. "You think that's fast, wait until Trent puts up the carolers."

Rowan frowned. "Live ones or statues?"

"Yes.

The bell above the Apothecary door jingled with mechanical politeness. Rowan looked up from behind the counter just as a sharply dressed woman stepped inside. She wore a bone-white coat, a clipboard tucked under one arm, and carried herself with the kind of posture that made people step out of her way without being asked.

"I'm looking for Rowan," she said, her tone clipped but practiced.

Rowan raised a brow. "That's me."

"I'm with the mayor's office," she continued. "Mayor Trent would like to commission you for a portrait. Pastels, full color. The image will be used for the annual Christmas card campaign."

Rowan blinked, unsure if this was a prank or some strange new form of community service "...Me?"

"He was very impressed by your Halloween work. The mayor values local talent—especially when it draws a crowd."

Before Rowan could answer, Lyra glided out from the back room like she'd been waiting for her cue.

"And what's the offer for our little art gremlin?"

The woman barely glanced her way. "One thousand dollars."

Lyra's smile was sugar-coated steel. "Two."

The assistant didn't blink. "Done."

That got Rowan's attention.

She reached into her bag and pulled out a folder, handing it to him like a business card. "The mayor is hoping to have it completed in the next two weeks. This includes the reference photo and image guidelines."

Rowan opened the folder. Inside was a high-gloss photo of Mayor Trent—chubby, balding, grinning like a used car commercial. He stood beside a woman in a sparkly red turtleneck, two teenage daughters in matching pea coats, and a golden retriever wearing a jingle bell collar.

Taped to the back of the photo was a typed compliance list:

**- Must be family-friendly
-No political symbols or messaging
-Holiday-neutral color palette
-Must include dog
-Mayor should appear confident and likable**

Rowan stared at it.

Lyra leaned over and squinted. "Is that hair?"

"I think it's glued on," Rowan muttered.

Lyra snorted. "Oh, this is going to be fun."

Rowan wasn't sure what was weirder—that the mayor wanted this done by him, or that they'd doubled the offer without blinking. Something was up. And if Mayor Trent wanted a perfect Christmas?

Rowan was going to give him exactly what he asked for. The door had barely shut behind the assistant before Lyra spun on her heel, eyes gleaming like she'd just been handed a loaded slingshot and a written invitation to use it.

"Family meeting!" she shouted, bolting toward the back room. Rowan barely had time to blink before he heard Talia's boots thundering down the stairs and Elysse calling, "If this is about the glitter incident again, I swear—"

Selene stepped out of the kitchen, wiping her hands on a tea towel. "What now?"

Lyra returned with the flair of someone delivering breaking news. "Rowan just got commissioned by the mayor. For the official Christmas card. Two thousand dollars. Full pastel portrait. The whole family—including the dog."

Talia's jaw dropped. "What?"

Elysse raised an eyebrow. "Two thousand?"

Rowan held up the folder. "He gave me a photo and a list. Very specific instructions."

Talia snatched the reference from his hand. "Is that Trent? With hair?"

"It's not real," Lyra whispered like it was a conspiracy.

Selene took the compliance list and scanned it in silence. "Flattering, confident, holiday-neutral..." She handed it back with a dry expression. "He's trying to look like a department store ad."

"I think he's trying to re brand," Elysse added thoughtfully. "That kind of polish usually means someone's planning a run at something."

"Re-election?" Rowan asked.

"Or something bigger," Selene murmured. "Which means this little drawing of yours might be seen by more than just Ashford Landing."

Rowan's eyes widened slightly. "So I'm political now?"

"No," Lyra said immediately. "You're a weapon."

Talia grinned. "A very expensive one."

Rowan looked around at their amused, calculating expressions, and suddenly realized—he hadn't just accepted a commission.

Later that afternoon, when the shop had thinned out and the girls were busy cycling through restock rotations and seasonal displays, Rowan slipped out with a quiet, "Be right back," and returned twenty minutes later with a crisp new sketchpad and a case of pastels tucked under his arm.

He didn't say much—just gave a little nod to Selene as he passed through the main room and headed straight for the back.

The workroom at the rear of the Apothecary was quiet, its long oak table scattered with scraps of parchment, dried herbs, bits of twine, and a few abandoned tea mugs. He cleared a space in the corner, dragging a stool into place and setting the sketchpad down like it was something sacred.

For a few seconds, he just stared at the blank page, it almost stared back. Smug; like it already knew how much pressure it carried.

Then he opened the folder, propped the glossy photo of Mayor Trent and his overly curated family beside him, and set the compliance list gently off to the side—just far enough to ignore.

He opened the pastels.

Chose a deep red.

Then, slowly, methodically, he began to draw.

Chapter Thirty — The Portrait

By the end of November, Ashford Landing had been fully consumed by what Talia called "Christmas Glory" and what Rowan quietly referred to as "the holiday monster that eats Halloween and doesn't chew." Even the gutters sparkled with leftover glitter. Rowan swore the pine garlands were multiplying overnight, creeping like ivy up railings and mailboxes. The town smelled like peppermint oil and fake snow. Overnight, the town had transformed.

Pumpkins, brooms and paper bats gave way to garlands of pine and strings of oversized bulbs in red, white, and gold. Every lamppost wore a velvet bow. Storefronts glowed with fairy lights. Animatronic reindeer twitched mechanically in display windows. The coffee shop offered six different kinds of peppermint beverages, and even the bookstore had swapped its usual banner for a sign that read "Stories to Warm Your Winter Soul" in hand-lettered calligraphy.

Above it all, hanging from the lamppost at the center of town, was Mayor Trent's face printed on a twelve-foot banner. He was smiling, arms folded across a red turtleneck. The words Ashford Landing Believes in Holiday Cheer! curled above his bald spot like a halo. The canvas flapped faintly in the wind, just enough to make the printed smile seem like it was twitching. Rowan had to pass under it every morning like a medieval subject beneath a royal crest—if the royal crest had an uncanny, retouched smirk and jingle bells. He'd gotten very good at not looking up.

Down in the cellar of the Apothecary, he hauled a heavy wooden crate onto the bottom step and paused to catch his breath. The scent of cedar, vanilla, and fresh-cut soap drifted up from the open lid like it was trying to lure him into a commercial. From the top of the stairs, Lyra peered down, one arm resting dramatically against the doorframe.

"This counts as strength training," she called helpfully. "We're multitasking."

Rowan looked up, deadpan. "You say that like you're doing it too." The cellar was cold and slightly damp, the scent of earth mixing with the sharper tang of cedar and soap. Rowan wiped a smear of wax off his sleeve as he hefted the crate.

"I'm doing the supervision part," she said, waving vaguely. "It's a very niche skill set."

Talia appeared behind her, holding a thermos and wearing the exact expression of someone preparing to cause problems on purpose. "You've been standing there for fifteen minutes."

"I am the support team."

"You're a loaf with legs."

"Bold words from someone who failed the wreath display challenge yesterday," Lyra replied, placing a hand over her heart. "Truly, you live without shame."

Talia handed Rowan the thermos as he reached the top step. "Hot cider. You earn it by not letting her convince you to dead-lift soap."

Rowan took it with a quiet "Thanks," and glanced toward Lyra, who sniffed. "I was gonna give him tea," she muttered.

"Sure you were."

After the soaps were shelved and Lyra had wandered off claiming "supervisory fatigue," Rowan retreated to the back room of the Apothecary. The door clicked softly behind him. The waxy surface of the table stuck faintly under his elbow. He brushed away a sprinkle of dried rosemary that crumbled like paper.

The candle prototypes flickered as he passed, one flame guttering from a hidden draft. Sunlight spilled in through the side window, cutting across the long table cluttered with parchment scraps, boxes of labels, a chipped mortar, and three half-finished candle prototypes—one of which still had a wick floating in liquid wax.

He cleared a space with the methodical rhythm of someone buying time. Then he sat down, pulled out the sketchpad and the folder, and opened them both.

Mayor Trent's picture stared up at him, plastic and perfect. That forced grin. The carefully posed family. The dog looked like the only one not faking it.

"Why me?" Rowan said aloud, almost to the photo.

"Because you're in right now," came Lyra's voice from the doorway.

He looked up to see her leaning one shoulder against the frame, arms crossed, eyes glittering with amusement.

"You're mysterious. Brooding. Talented. A little feral. The tourists are eating it up."

Talia appeared behind her, sipping something from a tall cup with cinnamon foam. "You're the spooky art kid with good cheekbones. It's very marketable."

Rowan stared. "Lyra literally acts like a witch. Looks like one. Why am I the one everyone's talking about?"

Lyra smiled like she'd been waiting for that question. "I want them to talk," she said. "I control the narrative. You don't."

"You also don't randomly light things on fire," Talia added, raising an eyebrow. "Rowan does."

"I didn't mean to," he muttered.

"That's why it's interesting," Lyra said with a wink.

Rowan scowled and looked back at the photo. "It's just... weird. I didn't do anything special. I'm not—"

"You survived," Lyra interrupted, this time softer. "That's more than most."

She stepped back, disappearing into the shop with a rustle of her coat. Talia lingered for a beat longer.

"You're not a story, Rowan. You're a spark. And sparks get noticed."

Then she followed after Lyra, leaving him alone with the dog, the mayor, and a page that hadn't been drawn on yet.

The next two weeks blurred together. Mornings began the same—cold, crisp, and laced with the scent of clove and pine drifting in from the town square. Rowan helped with the morning shop setup, lighting candles in the windows, restocking the seasonal soap displays, and sweeping the stoop clear of snow-dusted leaves. By now, he knew where every box went, which displays needed fluffing, and exactly how many jars of clove salve they had left without checking inventory.

Then came the caricatures. Not the rush like Halloween, just a steady trickle—locals and shop regulars who claimed they "just wanted something fun," but always seemed to mention the mayor's portrait in the same breath. Some brought their pets. One older woman brought a ceramic owl. Rowan drew them all without complaint, his fingers moving on instinct.

But his mind? Always on the portrait.

The back room became his second heartbeat. Between customers, between shelves, between bites of lunch—he was there. Staring down the photo. Layering color. Softening edges. Redrawing the mayor's mouth three times until it looked less like a smirk and more like a campaign promise.

He got used to the way chalk dust clung to his fingertips no matter how often he washed his hands. He got used to Lyra poking her head in once a day to offer dry commentary and Talia leaving snacks with handwritten notes like "artist fuel, do not throw away." Even Elysse dropped by once, looked at the half-finished piece, and simply said, "That dog deserves better," before walking out again.

By the end of the second week, the portrait was nearly done. The daughters looked polished. The wife had just the right amount of soft shading around her eyes. The dog was perfect. The mayor?

Rowan had redrawn his face five times. No matter how he softened the jawline or shaded the eyes, the face kept curdling into something smug. The more he tried to fix it, the more the smile looked like a warning.

Not because he couldn't get the angle right. He could.

It was the expression.

He couldn't make it look honest.

Tire tracks cut dark lines through the fresh snow, steam rising faintly from the hood. The car didn't hum—it loomed. Out stepped the woman in the wool coat, clipboard in hand like a badge of rank.

The front door opened with a click, and a woman in a wool coat and matching gloves stepped out, clutching a clipboard with the same precision as the first time she'd entered. This time, she didn't even bother stepping inside. She just stood near the passenger door and waited.

Rowan stood frozen in the middle of the shop, sketchpad still tucked under one arm, portrait wrapped carefully in brown paper and twine beside him. The others had gone still too, like a spell had settled over the room.

"Why's he here himself?" Lyra asked from behind the counter, her tone suddenly too casual.

Talia was already peeking out the window. "Oh, he brought press."

"Of course he did," Elysse muttered. "God forbid a moment pass without narrative control."

Selene came in from the back hallway, drying her hands on a towel. She stopped dead when she saw the limo.

Then she looked at Rowan. His grip on the sketchpad had tightened, knuckles white.

"Do you want me to go out with you?" she asked gently.

Rowan didn't answer right away. He stepped forward slowly, picked up the wrapped portrait, and held it like it might crack in two.

Then he nodded.

The bell jingled softly as they stepped outside together. Cold air hit his cheeks like static. The woman with the clipboard gave them a polite, practiced smile and opened the rear door.

Mayor Trent stepped out wearing a deep green coat with a plaid scarf thrown just so over one shoulder. His smile was glossy. His hair had definitely been touched up since the photo.

But it wasn't the mayor Rowan was looking at.

It was the row of reporters across the street.

Tripods. Microphones. Flashbulbs already going off.

He stiffened.

Selene's hand touched the center of his back—calm, steady, grounding.

But his voice still cracked when he turned toward her and whispered—

Rowan's pulse thrummed loud in his ears. He adjusted his grip on the wrapped portrait. Then—quiet, "Mom... there's cameras."

Chapter Thirty-One — The Speech

The mayor and his family stood outside the limo, smiling like the cameras owed them money. Mayor Trent's grin was broad and gleaming, the kind perfected over years of ribbon cuttings and county fair appearances. His wife wore a red coat that matched his scarf exactly, her makeup flawless in the cold light. The two daughters posed in matching peacoats and ankle boots, holding their arms just close enough to suggest familial affection without risking rumpling the aesthetic. And the dog—fluffy, golden, with a perfect red velvet bow around his neck—sat at the mayor's feet like he'd been trained by a film crew.

The whole family looked plastic. Their coats didn't wrinkle when they moved. Their smiles held too long. The daughters tilted their heads in sync, and the mayor's scarf caught the light like it had been steamed before the photo op. Every movement—the wave, the smile, the reach to fix a scarf—was executed with choreographed grace. Like this had all been rehearsed. Maybe it had.

Rowan stood just behind Selene on the Apothecary stoop, the wrapped portrait under his arm, and tried not to fidget. One of the photographers shouted for the mayor to look "a little more festive." The mayor responded by lifting the dog into his arms and laughing with just enough throw to his voice that it echoed off the building behind them. Selene leaned over slightly and said out of the corner of her mouth, "If he starts handing out candy canes we're walking back inside."

Rowan didn't laugh. He couldn't. Because in that moment, he realized this wasn't about a portrait. It was about him.

Mayor Trent took the portrait from Rowan with the kind of reverence usually reserved for newborns and local sports trophies. "Oh, this is stunning," he said, turning toward the cameras, his voice raised just enough to carry. "Absolutely stunning. This young man is a gift to our community."

He held up the portrait—still wrapped—and posed for a few quick flashes before carefully tucking it under one arm like he planned to cradle it for the rest of the season. Rowan shifted his weight. Cold air bit at his knuckles, but it was the numbness under his skin—the way the world tilted, hollow and buzzing—that made him curl his fingers tighter around the wrapping.

"Now," the mayor continued, stepping up onto the low stone planter just beside the Apothecary's sign, "I'd like to say a few words, if I may." He didn't wait for permission. The crowd—small, mostly press, a few curious townspeople—leaned forward as he cleared his throat, smiled wide, and began.

"Ashford Landing is built on tradition," he said. "On community. On legacy. And no season represents that better than Christmas. It's a time for family. For generosity. For unity."

He gestured toward Rowan with a kind, fatherly smile that immediately felt wrong. "This holiday, I want to do something meaningful. Something that reflects what this town is truly about." The dog gave a perfectly timed woof and was promptly patted on the head.

"I want to thank Rowan, not just for his beautiful artwork, but for reminding all of us what it means to come together. He's the reason we remember that giving someone a home—giving them a place to belong—is the greatest gift of all."
Rowan stared at him. This wasn't part of the agreement. He hadn't signed up for this.

The mayor's smile didn't waver, but he raised a hand and nodded toward someone off to the side. The assistant stepped forward, taking the spot beside him with the ease of someone who had done this a hundred times before. Her tone was soft, professional, and rehearsed to the syllable.

"Many of you may not know Rowan's story," she began. "A young boy with extraordinary talent, surviving on his own for years. No home. No family. No guidance. Just... potential."

Rowan froze; his palms started to sweat, even in the cold. He hadn't told anyone those things—not in those words—and hearing them echoed back felt like someone reading his diary through a bullhorn. He glanced toward Selene, but her expression was unreadable. Not angry. Not surprised. Just... quiet.

"And then," the assistant continued, her voice swelling with gentle reverence, "along came Selene—a local business owner, healer, and pillar of this community—who opened her home and her heart. She took him in, not knowing where he came from, not needing to."

The cameras snapped. Flashes burst. The white bursts burned behind Rowan's eyelids. Each click of the shutter landed like a knock on his rib cage.

"It's people like Selene," the assistant said, with a smile just soft enough to pass for humility, "who remind us that kindness isn't seasonal. It's who we are."

The mayor clapped lightly, then picked up again without missing a beat.

"And in the spirit of that kindness, I'm thrilled to announce—"

Rowan already knew what was coming. He just didn't know how much it was going to hurt.

"I shall personally see to it that Rowan is adopted by Christmas!" He said with a smile.

The crowd cheered.

Selene didn't flinch. She didn't shout, didn't bristle, didn't even blink. She just offered the mayor a smile so perfectly measured, so carefully constructed, it could've been bottled and sold as diplomacy. Then, without a single word to the press, she placed a hand on Rowan's shoulder and said, "Let's go inside."

The door closed behind them with a soft chime—and a hard line between outside performance and inside reality. Inside, chaos was already in full swing.

"Oh my gods," Talia hissed, pacing behind the counter. "Did he just announce a private family decision like it was a town raffle?"

"I think we just witnessed political theater," Lyra said, draped dramatically over an armchair, clearly delighted. "Very well staged. I give it four out of five exploding ornaments."

"You're not helping!" Talia snapped.

"Neither is the mayor," Lyra quipped. "He just told the whole town we're adopting Rowan like it was his idea."

From the back room, Elysse didn't even glance up from her notebook. "He said he'd personally oversee it," she corrected, her voice neutral. "Which means he wants credit, not responsibility."

Lyra clapped once. "Ah yes, classic politician."

Talia groaned into both hands.

Rowan just stood in the middle of it all—confused, exhausted, and weirdly comforted by the fact that no matter what the mayor said outside, in here, things still made sense. Or at least, they made chaos. He sighed as the scent of mint and honey from the winter candles had settled thick in the air. Somewhere, a kettle clicked off. The familiar clutter of books, herbs, and half-finished potion jars grounded him.

Selene walked past them all, slipping off her coat with quiet grace. She paused only once—beside Elysse.

"I want every name that was on that permit request," she said calmly.

Elysse's pen didn't pause. Her handwriting flowed across the page, measured and sharp as she turned a page. "Already compiling the list."

Chapter Thirty-Two — The Conversation

The clink of forks on ceramic was louder than it should've been. No music played. Even the kettle's whistle earlier had sounded reluctant, like it didn't want to start the day either. Everyone was waiting for someone else to explain what had happened the day before.

Selene made eggs. Talia poured coffee. Lyra stood at the counter cutting a grapefruit with the kind of concentration usually reserved for surgery. Rowan sat at the table, shoulders a little higher than usual, eyes on the steam curling up from his mug. He picked at the hem of his sleeve without realizing it, each thread like a distraction he couldn't quite pull loose.

Elysse walked in last, a neatly clipped stack of papers tucked under one arm and a pen between her fingers. She didn't sit right away. The papers hit the table with a sharp thud that sent a ripple through everyone's posture. Even the grapefruit stopped mid-slice.

"We've been signed up," she said dryly, "for every form of government assistance available in the tri-state area."

Talia blinked. "What?"

Elysse held up the top form. "Subsidized energy. State-sponsored meal programs. Winter clothing vouchers. Dental."

Lyra squinted. "Did you sign us up for that?"

"No," Elysse said, flipping a page. "Mayor Trent's office did. Yesterday. Retroactively. Effective immediately."

A crooked breath caught in Rowan's throat, halfway between a scoff and a shiver. He wasn't sure which direction it wanted to go.

Elysse continued. "According to the attached note, these are to ensure Rowan has a 'proper transition' into a household environment. As if he wandered in from the woods."

"Oh, he's officially a forest goblin now," Lyra said, biting into her grapefruit.

Talia looked genuinely offended. "We make his meals from scratch."

"I do his hair," Lyra added. "It's a public service."

Elysse slid the whole stack toward Selene, who read the first page with an expression like she was reading the weather report: unbothered, but calculating.

"Any action required on our part?" she asked.

Elysse shook her head. "No. It's mostly performative. But there's a public record now. The town believes this process is officially underway."

Rowan shifted in his seat. He hadn't said a word yet, but his hands had stopped moving. Selene looked at him then—not concerned, not prying. Just waiting. He didn't meet her eyes. Rowan cleared his throat softly. Selene glanced toward him again, this time a little more focused.

"I didn't mean to cause—" he started.

"You didn't," she said immediately.

But he kept going anyway. "—any trouble. I just wanted to help. With the portrait. I didn't think he'd—"

"You didn't cause this," Selene said again, firmer this time.

Rowan looked down at his plate. He nodded, but the eggs on his plate had gone cold and untouched. He nudged them once with his fork like they might answer for him.

Before the silence could stretch, Elysse cut in, flipping to a new page in her stack. "We also have a home inspection next week," she said matter-of-factly. "Child Protective Services, Monday morning."

Talia dropped her fork. "Are you serious?"

Lyra muttered something under her breath that sounded vaguely like a curse in a dead language.

"Standard procedure," Elysse went on. "They're not questioning us—they're verifying us. Because now that the mayor has decided to turn this into a local fairytale, the state would very much like to be involved."

Rowan looked up. "They're coming here?"

"Yes," Elysse said. "We've been flagged as a household taking in a minor without prior approval. Never mind that he's been here for months and thriving. What matters is that people noticed. And once the government notices, everyone else feels the need to act like they were watching all along."

Rowan sank back slightly in his chair. His appetite, what little he had, vanished. He felt Selene's eyes on him again—still calm, still unreadable—but she didn't speak. He wasn't sure if that made it better or worse.

The moment Elysse said home inspection, both Talia and Lyra jolted into action.

"Oh no," Talia said, already halfway to standing. "No no no no. We have to hide the curse shelf."

"The what?" Rowan asked.

Lyra ignored him. "We have to hide a lot more than that. The charm drawer, the talking mirror, the soap that bites—"

"The dagger in the coat closet," Talia added.

"The mirror in the upstairs hall."

"All the mirrors upstairs."

"Oh my gods," Lyra said, spinning toward Selene. "Do you think they'll bring a dog? You know—the kind that sniffs?"

Talia immediately looked at the floor like she was seeing it in a new light. "We'll need salt. Probably three kinds."

Rowan blinked. "What would it be sniffing for?"

"Demon residue."

Selene, calmly stacking plates, said, "There is no demon residue."

"But if there were, we'd need to clean it," Lyra insisted.

"I'll re-ward the pantry," Talia muttered, already running down a mental checklist. "I swear that cauldron moved on its own yesterday."

"That's because you left it half-full of nightshade and shame," Elysse deadpanned.

The volume crested like a wave about to break. Books were being pulled off shelves. Talia was mid-sprint toward the upstairs mirror. Then Selene moved. Selene placed a firm hand on the stack of papers. "No one is hiding anything. We're not doing anything wrong."

Lyra threw both hands in the air. "That is objectively untrue, and you know it."

"You're not helping," Talia snapped.

"I'm never helping," Lyra replied. "I'm inspirational, not logistical."

Rowan sat in silence as the argument spiraled around him —chaotic, loud, familiar. For a moment, he wasn't sure whether to laugh or bolt. Instead, he excused himself quietly and slipped toward the hallway.

The din of argument swelled—Lyra and Talia tossing snark and panic back and forth like it was a competitive sport.

"We have three shelves of spell ingredients in Latin," Talia was saying. "Do you think CPS speaks Latin?"

"Honestly?" Lyra said, pausing mid-rant. "I kind of hope they do. I have questions."

Selene didn't raise her voice. She didn't need to. She simply picked up her keys from the hook by the door, turned, and said, "We're opening the Apothecary."

That stopped everyone. Talia froze mid-sip of coffee. Lyra slowly lowered her grapefruit half like it had personally betrayed her. Elysse looked up with quiet approval, already folding the paperwork and tucking it back into a folder.

Rowan blinked. "You're... just going to open the shop?" he asked.

Selene looked at him calmly. "Yes. Because it's Saturday. And on Saturdays, we open the shop."

Then she walked to the door, pulled on her coat, and stepped out into the cold morning air. Calm, deliberate, unshaken. Rowan found himself standing, not because he decided to, but because somehow, gravity started obeying her instead.

Chapter Thirty-Three — The Rush.

The next few days hit like a sleigh crash. The moment Mayor Trent's speech went public, Ashford Landing collectively decided that the Apothecary was now a holiday destination. Not just for candles or salves—but for spectacle. By Tuesday, the line stretched out the door and wrapped around the corner. Tourists and locals came bundled in scarves, hats, and vague curiosity.

A few clutched lists. Others had cameras half-hidden in coat pockets. One woman stood in the doorway and pretended to shop while clearly scanning the room for someone specific. Outside, the cold pressed noses red and made mittens clumsy. Inside, warmth wrapped too tight—sugar-sweet and stifling, like a cinnamon roll no one asked for.

"Do you think that's him?" whispered a man by the soaps, not whispering at all. "The one who drew the mayor's portrait?"

Rowan was behind the counter, helping Talia restock the seasonal displays. His shoulders were hunched slightly, like he was expecting to be tackled by attention at any moment.

"Rowan!" someone called brightly. "Would you mind signing my receipt?"

He blinked. "What?" he stiffened like he'd been asked to autograph a baby, unsure of whether this was a prank or not.

"It's just—my husband said you're going to be famous, and it'd be fun to have a signed copy, just in case!"

Before he could answer, Talia leaned over and very politely said, "Receipts go in the trash, Margaret. Come buy a candle if you want a collectible."

In the corner, Lyra sat on a stool behind the cash register, watching the chaos with the contentment of a cat watching fish in a tank. "I should've started charging for photos," she muttered.

"Don't," Elysse said from behind a clipboard. "We're one 'miracle boy' headline away from a full investigation."

Outside, someone snapped a photo through the window. The flash left a ghost reflection across the glass, briefly framing Rowan like a saint in stained glass.

"But think of the marketing," Lyra replied dreamily. "Holiday chaos. Magic soap. Adopted child artist. We'd sell out before Christmas."

The Apothecary was a war zone. Not in the usual way—no spilled vials, no magical misfires, not even a mid-shift candle collapse. No, this was a very different kind of battle. This was a brutal, cheer-soaked ambush of kindness. The kind that made Rowan want to crawl into a display of eucalyptus bath bombs and never come out.

"Sweetheart," said Mrs. Rigsby, pressing something into his hand. "It's not much, just a little something to help with the adoption costs."

He blinked at the crumpled twenty. "Oh. Um. Thank you—"

But she was already gone, replaced by Mr. Havers, who insisted on purchasing nine peppermint soaps and refusing the change.

Lyra leaned against the counter, arms folded, watching the chaos like it was performance art. "This town is terrifying."

"I'm going to cry," Rowan whispered.

"Don't," she replied. "They'll give you more money."

Across the room, someone dropped a folded check on the register like it was a wedding gift. "For the boy!" they called. "Bless his heart!"

Talia shrieked from behind the candle display. "SOMEONE JUST SLIPPED CASH INTO MY WAX!"

Selene, standing by the front display table, looked like she was trying to smile through dental surgery. "Everyone," she said gently, "we appreciate your support, but—"

"I brought baked goods!" shouted a woman from the doorway, pushing in a tray stacked with cupcakes frosted to look like snowmen. "For the family!"

"We're not a charity," Selene added, louder this time.

Someone placed a gift card in front of Rowan labeled "For Warm Winter Clothes and Maybe Therapy?"

"I hate it here," he muttered.

Elysse appeared beside him like a ghost. "They're all in the spirit, apparently."

"The spirit of what?" Rowan asked. "Pity?"

"No," Lyra said, voice bone-dry. "The spirit of aggressively overcompensating for watching you dig through a dumpster six months ago."

Rowan flopped forward onto the counter and groaned. "I should've drawn him ugly."

Selene stepped out the back door and closed it quietly behind her. The cold hit instantly—sharp, bracing, clean. The kind of winter air that cleared your lungs whether you wanted it to or not. For a moment, she just stood there, eyes closed, the distant noise of the shop muffled by the door. Then—

"I have to admit," came a voice from the shadows, smooth and amused, "I didn't expect the bake sale."

Lucian stepped out from behind the far corner of the building, gloved hands tucked neatly behind his back. His silhouette slid into view like it belonged to the fog—shadowy, self-satisfied, and wearing smugness like an overcoat.

Selene didn't turn. "Watching from the alley now?" she said flatly.

"Someone has to keep an eye on things," he replied. "The boy is drawing quite the crowd."

He paced slowly toward her, the snow crunching faintly beneath his boots. "You really think this is sustainable?" Lucian asked, tone light, like they were discussing the weather. "Keeping him in a shop full of trinkets and old magic? Letting him play house while he glows like a beacon every time he gets emotional?"

Selene turned to face him now, gaze steady. "He's a child."

Lucian tilted his head. "No. He's a weapon. And not one you can control forever."

For a moment, neither of them spoke. The wind stirred the edges of Selene's coat. Lucian smiled faintly, eyes narrowing. "You always did love lost causes."

The wind whistled past, stealing the warmth from her collar. Selene didn't flinch. Lost causes had a way of finding her. And she'd never been good at letting go.

Chapter Thirty-Four — The Quiet Shift

The air in the shop was thick with pine and clove and the sugary cling of too many holiday candles, but when Selene stepped through the door, it felt like the temperature dropped three degrees.

The bells above the door gave their usual cheerful jingle, but something in her step was a little too precise, a little too quiet. She didn't speak. Didn't scold or direct or even sigh. She just slipped off her gloves, placed them gently beside the register, and glanced toward the back of the store.

That's when her eyes met Rowan's. She didn't say anything. She didn't have to. He could see it. Not worry. Not fear. Strain. That sharp, cold tension that lived in her shoulders and behind her eyes when something had gone wrong but she hadn't decided how to handle it yet.

So he did the only thing he knew how to do. He started moving. He grabbed the bag of dried pine sachets and began restocking the scent wall. He ran the register without waiting for someone to ask. He offered recommendations to customers before they had a chance to start the "bless your heart" routine. When an elderly woman tried to hand him a holiday card with a twenty-dollar bill inside, he smiled politely, handed it back, and said, "Ma'am, I'm not a donation bin." And then helped her pick out three soaps like it never happened.

Lyra raised an eyebrow behind the counter but said nothing. Talia mouthed Are you okay? across the store. He just nodded and kept moving. Faster. Sharper. Focused. Because something was wrong. And if he couldn't fix it, he could at least make himself useful.

Dinner that night came in paper bags. The lights overhead cast a soft yellow glow on the worn wood of the kitchen table, its surface cluttered with open takeout containers and mismatched chopsticks. Outside, the frost clung to the windows in delicate starbursts, blurring the edges of the world. Talia had called in the order on the way home, and now the table was scattered with takeout containers: sesame chicken, lo mein, spring rolls in waxy paper sleeves, and a tub of something suspiciously green that no one claimed ordering.

The silence came in waves. Selene sat at the end of the table, quietly dividing a portion of rice like she was performing surgery. Elysse ate with her usual precision, reading something between bites. Talia stabbed her chopsticks into a pile of noodles like they'd personally wronged her. Only Lyra looked at peace, with one leg tucked beneath her and a spring roll in each hand.

"So," she said cheerfully, "how many cupcakes did we end up with today? Fifteen? Twenty?"

"Seventeen," Elysse replied without looking up. "Not counting the ones Talia stepped on in the back hallway."

"They were in the middle of the floor!" Talia snapped. "What kind of psychopath ambushes people with cupcakes?"

"Suburban women with something to prove," Lyra said around a mouthful of food. "It's the frosting. Sugar amplifies intent."

Rowan's lips twitched, the smallest breath slipping past his nose like a secret trying to escape. His container of sesame chicken sat half-finished in front of him. He wasn't hungry anymore, but he wasn't about to say that out loud. He glanced at Selene. She hadn't said a word since they got home. Not cold, not angry. Just... measured. Like she was still thinking. Still calculating. Still watching. And for some reason, that made him want to be smaller. Quieter. Better.

"Rowan," Talia said gently, nudging a second egg roll in his direction. "You good?"

He nodded quickly and shoved a bite of rice into his mouth before she could ask again.

Across the table, Lyra pointed her spring roll at him. "Blink twice if the cupcake mafia got to you."

After dinner, the house settled into its usual nighttime rhythm—dishes stacked, lights dimmed, slippers scuffed across hardwood floors. Rowan didn't go up to his room. He lingered in the hallway, pretending to look at nothing in particular until Selene passed by on her way to the kitchen. She stopped without needing to be asked.

"Want to take a walk?" she asked softly.

He nodded. They stepped out the front door together into the chill. No words, just breath fogging in the cold. Gravel crunched underfoot with each step, the only sound aside from the far-off creak of a shifting tree branch. The moonlight filtered through bare limbs, casting tangled shadows across the path. It wasn't far—just far enough that the house lights faded behind them. The moon hung low. Everything smelled like frost and pine and the tail end of autumn. They walked in silence for a while. Then Rowan said it, quiet but sharp as a spark.

"Is it because of my magic?"

Selene slowed. Not stopped—just slowed. Rowan stared straight ahead, his arms folded tight across his chest.

"You don't have to lie," he added quickly. "I just... I need to know. Is that why you took me in?" The word tasted bitter in his mouth. He didn't look at her. He didn't want to see the answer coming. But Selene didn't rush to fill the silence. She never did. When she finally spoke, her voice was calm. Clear.

"No." She let the word settle before continuing. "You being a witch isn't why I took you in. It's not why I let you stay. It's not why I made you a room, or why I remember how you take your eggs, or why there's a hook for your coat by the door."

Rowan's breath caught.

"I took you in," she said, "because I saw a boy who was surviving when he should have been living. Because you reminded me of someone I used to be. And because... the moment I saw you, I knew you belonged with us."

Rowan opened his mouth, but the words stuck. He didn't know what to say. So he just stood there, nodding, eyes burning in the cold.

Selene turned to face him, her expression soft but steady. "Your magic is a part of you," she said. "But it's not the reason you're mine."

They stood there in the quiet, the cold settling gently around them like a second skin. He swallowed hard, his voice barely rising above the wind. "What if I become like him?"

Selene didn't ask who he meant. She didn't need to.

"You won't," she said.

"You don't know that."

"I do." He shook his head. "He's powerful. He's smart. He's... careful. And he's been following me since before I knew who he was."

Selene was quiet for a moment. Then she said,

"Lucian's been more involved in your life than you realize."

Rowan turned toward her, alarm sparking in his chest.

"What do you mean?"

144

"I mean he's been watching. For years. Keeping distance. But watching." She didn't say it like an accusation. She said it like a fact.

"That doesn't mean he's the one who raised you."

Rowan looked down at his shoes, breath forming clouds in the air.

"I don't want to end up like him," he whispered.

Selene placed a hand on his shoulder. "You don't have to," she said. "The difference between Lucian and you isn't your magic. It's your choices."

He didn't answer right away. But after a while, he nodded. Just once. And when she turned to walk back toward the house, he followed.

Chapter Thirty-Five — The Visit

CPS was scheduled to arrive at 10:00 a.m. At 7:43 a.m., the house was in full military operation.

"This is a government inspection," Elysse said, setting down her fourth cup of tea and unfurling a detailed checklist that stretched nearly to the floor. "Not a brunch. Not a festival. Not a test we can afford to fail."

Somewhere upstairs, a drawer slammed. The scent of burnt toast lingered in the hallway like smoke from a spell gone sideways. A bathroom door creaked open and shut again, rapid-fire.

"I feel like we could bribe them with brunch," Lyra offered from the stairs, holding a muffin in one hand and a candle in the other. "Just hypothetically."

"No bribes," Elysse said. "No magic. And for the love of sanity, no unlicensed soap."

"I feel like that one was targeted," Talia muttered, arms full of throw pillows.

Elysse pointed without looking. "Living room: inviting, but not staged. Throw blanket on the armrest. Candles lit, but only two—battery-powered."

"Battery-powered candles are for cowards," Lyra muttered two steps from the top with muffin crumbs on her dress.

"Kitchen: spotless. Leave out a loaf of bread, half-sliced. Fruit in the bowl. Nothing exotic. No pomegranates, no figs, and for gods' sake, no jars with floating eyeballs this time."

"That was one time," Talia hissed.

"That jar blinked," Elysse snapped.

Selene, calm as ever, passed through the hallway with a fresh pot of coffee like the eye of a hurricane. "Front room's ready," she said. "I'll handle the introductions."

"Good," Elysse said. "Keep it warm. Not cold, not overly friendly. You're stable, not desperate."

"I am stable."

"I know. But make them believe it in writing."

Rowan, meanwhile, was already dressed, hair brushed, room cleaned, and attempting to look like a normal teenager who hadn't spent the last twenty-four hours preparing for a government inspection with witches. He peeked into the kitchen, where Elysse was now adjusting a strategically placed cutting board to look "authentically used."

"Do I... say anything?" he asked.

"Yes," she said. "Be polite. Be articulate. And if they ask you if you feel safe here—"

"I do."

"Say it exactly like that."

The knock came at 10:02 a.m. sharp. Selene opened the door with the kind of grace reserved for headmistresses and courtroom legends. Calm. Measured. Perfectly composed.

On the doorstep stood a woman in a gray blazer holding a tablet, a man with a camera slung around his neck, and—of course —Mayor Trent, grinning like he'd planned this personally.

"Good morning!" he beamed. "Thought I'd tag along, you know, for moral support. And our friends at the Ashford Landing Gazette wanted to do a human-interest piece on all the wonderful things happening in our town!"

Selene's smile was the kind that made wine curdle. "How thoughtful." her hand, still on the doorknob, tightened slightly. You could practically hear the restraint in her jaw.

The CPS worker, whose badge read Ms. Callahan, offered a polite nod. "We don't usually do visits with press present, but the mayor assured me it would be a quick photo, and he'd remain outside during the interview process."

"I'm very good at staying out of the way," Mayor Trent said, already stepping inside.

Selene moved just enough to block him. "I'm sure you are."

Elysse appeared behind her with an uncanny ability to read a room and ruin someone's day. "Mayor Trent, thank you for coming. We've prepared a folder of documents for CPS and another one for your 'human interest' team. Feel free to wait outside. Or in traffic."

The mayor chuckled like she'd told a great joke and retreated to the porch. The photographer gave Selene a sheepish shrug and followed.

Inside, Ms. Callahan surveyed the entryway with professional precision. She was clearly someone who'd seen her share of staged homes and scrubbed-over secrets—and she didn't look particularly impressed by anything.

"Can I speak with Rowan first?" she asked.

Selene nodded once and gestured toward the living room. Rowan sat on the edge of the couch, cushion barely dipped under his weight. The battery-powered candles hummed quietly in their fake flicker, casting soft shadows that felt like they were holding their breath.

"Hi," he said, offering his most awkward smile.

Ms. Callahan smiled gently back. "I just have a few questions, Rowan. This won't take long."

Behind her, Lyra mouthed dramatically from the hallway: Act normal.

Rowan tried very, very hard not to laugh.

Ms. Callahan settled into the armchair across from Rowan, tablet in hand, stylus at the ready. She gave him a reassuring smile —the kind that had clearly been practiced in a mirror.

"Rowan, I'd like to start with a few simple questions, alright?"

He nodded, folding his hands in his lap.

"Do you feel safe here?"

"Yes."

"Oh, I bet he does!" Mayor Trent called from just outside the open front door. "Selene's done wonders with him—just wonders."

Rowan's eye twitched.

Ms. Callahan didn't acknowledge the interruption. "Do you have your own space in the home?"

"Yes. I have a room."

"With clothes and personal belongings?"

"Yes."

"He didn't even have a coat before he moved in," the mayor added, as if narrating a tragic PBS special. "Now look at him! Practically glowing."

Lyra coughed loud enough to be heard from the kitchen. Rowan wasn't sure if it was a laugh or a warning.

Ms. Callahan continued, barely blinking. "Do you feel supported emotionally?"

Rowan paused. That was trickier. But eventually, he said, "Yes. They've... helped. A lot."

"Beautiful," the mayor said. "Just beautiful. The power of found family!"

Selene didn't move. Didn't even look over. But the temperature in the room dropped by three degrees.

Ms. Callahan glanced up from her notes. "How are your relationships with the other household members?"

Rowan cleared his throat. "They're... loud. But they care. I like them."

The mayor, beaming now, leaned through the doorway with both thumbs up. "They adore him. And the dog! He gets along great with the family dog!"

"We have a cat" Rowan muttered.

Lyra's glare somehow floated from the hallway.

Ms. Callahan finally turned toward the mayor. "I'd like to continue the interview without outside commentary, if you don't mind."

The mayor chuckled and raised his hands. "Of course! Just so proud of the little guy."

Rowan buried his face in his hands.

Ms. Callahan stood, tablet in hand. "I'd like to do a brief walk-through of the home, if that's alright."

"Of course!" Selene said smoothly. "We'll begin with the kitchen."

Mayor Trent swept in ahead of her like a cruise director who'd been waiting for his moment. "Now this is where the magic happens! Metaphorically, of course!" He laughed like he'd made a joke. No one else did.

Selene led the way. Talia and Lyra flanked Rowan from both sides the moment the adults moved forward.

"You okay?" Talia whispered.

"No," he muttered. "I feel like I'm being sold on late night television."

"Don't worry," Lyra added, "I'll push him down the stairs if things get worse."

Up ahead, Ms. Callahan entered the kitchen and immediately began tapping notes on her tablet.

"The appliances are up to date," Selene said evenly. "We cook fresh meals daily."

Mayor Trent beamed. "I've had her cooking. Best stew in the county. Probably the tri-county area!"

"Is the refrigerator stocked?" Ms. Callahan asked.

Talia opened it dramatically, revealing neatly arranged containers, fresh produce, and one forgotten bottle of green soda rolling around the back.

"Plenty of food," she said. "No spells."

"Not anymore," Lyra muttered.

They moved through the dining room—Mayor Trent: "You can feel the family atmosphere in here!"—into the living room, where the battery-powered candles flickered like obedient little lies.

Ms. Callahan raised an eyebrow at the bookshelf. "All fiction," Elysse said from the shadows. "Filed by genre. Color coding is for the weak."

Upstairs, Rowan's room passed inspection with flying colors. His bed was made, his clothes put away, and the sketch of a dog he'd never owned tucked discreetly behind a pile of books.

"Very tidy for a teenager," Ms. Callahan noted.

"Oh, he's a special teen," the mayor gushed. "Keeps things clean, draws like a prodigy, survived on his own for three years. Just incredible resilience!"

Rowan stood in the doorway, arms crossed, actively trying to die.

In the hallway, Lyra casually leaned against a closet door—her shoulder pressed too firmly against it like she was holding something back—physically and emotionally. One boot tapped a little too deliberately. Her smile was the exact shape of plausible deniability.

"Nothing in here," she said before anyone could ask. "Just boring old winter coats. Some unmatched gloves. Definitely no enchanted taxidermy."

Ms. Callahan blinked. "...Excuse me?"

"I said umbrellas."

The second the front door closed behind Ms. Callahan and Mayor Trent, a heavy silence fell over the house. Then:

"OH MY GODS," Talia exploded, throwing both hands in the air. "We are going to JAIL."

"No we're not," Elysse said flatly.

"I blacked out during the kitchen inspection," Talia continued, pacing wildly. "Did I hide the moon salt? Did anyone hide the moon salt?!"

"You didn't," Lyra said, slamming the hallway closet shut. "But I ate the label, so legally it's just seasoning now."

Talia made a sound like a dying bird.

"I'll have you know," Lyra added, her voice now climbing into something ancient and furious, "that that man said the phrase 'moral uplift' while looking directly at my boots. My boots, Elysse!"

"I heard him," Elysse said, already pulling open her laptop. "I'm going to destroy his life with paperwork."

Rowan stood motionless in the middle of the room, wide-eyed, unsure whether to laugh or hide.

Selene exhaled slowly and walked to the center of the house. She knelt, touched the floorboards, and muttered something soft under her breath. They pulsed faintly beneath her touch. The air shifted—not colder or warmer, but clearer, like a held breath finally released. Rowan felt the tension drain from the walls, the weight slide from his chest. The house had been watching. And now, it blinked.

"I never want to do that again," he said.

"Congratulations," Lyra muttered, flopping face down onto the couch. "You've just survived your first government intrusion. Hope you enjoyed the trauma cupcakes."

Chapter Thirty-Six — Between

The day after the CPS visit felt like waking up from a very long, very weird dream. The walls didn't creak like they were holding their breath. The floorboards stopped whispering secrets with every step. Even the light felt looser, warmer, like the whole house had shrugged off its coat.

No more inspections. No more folders. No more pretending the family was anything other than a mildly chaotic coven held together by sarcasm, homemade lotion, and whatever gods still answered Selene's coffee prayers.

The air in the Apothecary lightened. Talia danced her way into the shop wearing a scarf the size of a throw blanket and declared that she would "only accept customers with good vibes and exact change."

Lyra finally stopped cursing in Norse—though she did hiss at a peppermint display that reminded her of Mayor Trent's cologne. And Selene? She smiled. Just once. Small, and only when she thought no one was looking. But Rowan saw it.

Life returned to normal. Or at least, Ashford Landing's version of it. Which meant retail hell.

The store exploded into a sensory overload of pine, cinnamon, clove, and relentless Christmas music. There were candle bundles tied with plaid ribbons, mini soap samplers shaped like snowflakes, and an entire table dedicated to "seasonal mood balancers"—which may or may not have contained trace amounts of anti-anxiety herbs.

The air felt thick with clove and cheer. Every breath came laced with pine needles and peppermint oil. The holiday playlist— looped to madness—sounded like jingle bells soaked in desperation.

They restocked shelves three times a day and still couldn't keep up. Customers barged in like gift-seeking hurricanes. Everyone wanted something "handmade," "local," and "authentically spiritual but not, like, weird."

By week two, Rowan was exhausted—hands stained with soap dye, glitter in his hair, three dollars in tips from a customer who mistook him for a holiday elf. He didn't even argue. He just put the money in his box and went back to organizing the shelves by scent and implied vibe.

Peppermint: Energizing.

Cedar: Grounding.

Clove: A little too judgmental for its own good.

It wasn't peaceful, but it was familiar.

If the inside of the Apothecary was chaos, the world outside Rowan's caricature tent had become its own brand of madness.

Every morning, before the shop even opened, there was a line. Locals. Tourists. Kids in snowflake sweaters. Grown men trying to act casual while handing over their $25 like it wasn't totally weird to commission a cartoon version of themselves for their cousin's Christmas gift.

By the end of the first week, Rowan had to move his setup to the edge of the courtyard just to keep the crowd from blocking the door. By the end of the second, someone set up a snack cart nearby—selling cider and cookies to people waiting for him.

He didn't complain. Not when his fingers cramped. Not when the wind stung his cheeks and made the charcoal smudge. Not when he started running on caffeine and stubbornness alone. He just kept drawing. Every sketch was sharp, clever, somehow exactly what each person wanted—even when they didn't know what that was. One old man laughed so hard at his caricature—complete with reindeer antlers and a nose like Rudolph's—he bought two and asked if Rowan would sign them both "To Grandma, from Santa."

But every morning, Rowan looked a little more tired. His eyes a little duller. His voice a little quieter.

Selene noticed. Of course she did. So did Elysse, who left an extra protein bar in his coat pocket every morning without saying a word. And Lyra, who started walking him home after dark in human form—never admitting that's what she was doing.

But Rowan never said anything about it. Not when they asked. Not when they hinted. Not even when Talia tried to pry it out of him with hot chocolate and aggressive affection. He just shook his head and said he was fine. Then picked up his pencil and went back to work.

Christmas Eve in Ashford Landing glowed like a snow globe turned upside down. The Apothecary was closed, the "back after the holidays" sign hanging proudly on the door. Inside the manor, the kitchen was filled with warmth—cookies cooling on parchment, cider simmering on the stove, and the scent of cinnamon clinging to everything like static.

But the mood was off. Subtle. Quiet. Frayed at the edges.
Talia leaned against the counter, arms crossed, watching the oven
with a furrowed brow that had nothing to do with cookies.
"He hasn't come down."
Lyra didn't look up from where she was casually eating raw sugar
cookie dough with a spoon. "He's working."
"He's always working."
Elysse sat at the table with a mug of black coffee, notebook closed
beside her, for once. "The light's been on every night."
Selene didn't speak. She was at the sink, drying her hands. Calm,
as always—but she had noticed too. Every night for the past two
weeks, Rowan's door had been locked. Every night, light glowed
beneath it long after the rest of the house had gone still. No
movement. No sound. Just light.

　　　She hadn't knocked. Hadn't pressed. But she noticed. The
warmth of the kitchen couldn't quite reach the hallway. His door
glowed at the end like a lantern in a forest—distant, unreachable,
and wrong.
"He's not sleeping," Talia muttered.
"He's running on pride and spite," Lyra replied, still chewing.
"Honestly, I respect it. But also, he's going to explode."
Elysse gave a small, tired smile. "No. He's going to give someone a
present. And then he'll explode."
"Alright," Lyra said, slamming her spoon into the sink with a sharp
clang, "that's enough."
Talia blinked. "Enough of what?"
"This silent martyr routine. He's been locking himself in there like
a cursed prince, and I'm over it."
Elysse didn't look up. "Don't do anything stupid."
"I'm his aunt," Lyra replied, already marching toward the hallway.
"Stupid is in the job description."
Selene opened her mouth to object, but Lyra was already gone—
boots stomping, scarf flying, muttering ancient curses under her
breath.

　　　Her eyes flashed, mouth set. The way she stormed down
the hall, she might as well have been wielding a sword instead of a
scarf. She didn't knock. Didn't ask. She raised one foot and kicked
the door in.
It slammed against the wall with a heavy crack, the sound
reverberating down the hall like thunder.
"Rowan!" she barked. "You can't keep—"

Then she stopped. Dead silent. The kind of silence that hit too fast to be casual.

Chapter Thirty-Seven — The Portrait Part 2

Her mouth opened. Closed. She blinked twice, like her brain had stalled somewhere between sarcasm and awe. Lyra stared at the portrait for a full five seconds before dramatically gasping.

Selene sat in the middle, perched in the old wicker chair from the sunroom. Her posture was steady, graceful—queen-like without trying. To her right stood Lyra, in her full human form— long hair as dark as midnight, eyes like emerald fire—holding her cat self cradled in one arm like a smug, enchanted loaf. To her left sat Elysse, eyes soft behind her glasses, caught in the moment of looking up from a book as if she'd just been asked a question she already knew the answer to. And behind her—laughing, head tilted back—was Talia, light caught in her red curls like flame, expression so vivid you could almost hear the joke that caused it.

In front of them, slightly off-center but drawn with incredible care, was Rowan. He sat cross-legged with a pencil tucked behind one ear and the hint of a smile that said yes, this is chaos... but it's mine.

"You sappy little—" Lyra turned so fast the scarf on her shoulder nearly spun off. "Is this why you've been avoiding everyone?! Because you were making us a feelings bomb?" Rowan flushed. "It's not a—"

"Don't you dare argue with me, young man." She jabbed a finger at him, eyes gleaming. "You either march downstairs with that drawing right now, or I will tell everyone that you've been holed up crafting a heartfelt Christmas surprise and you'll never know peace again."
He stared at her. She stared back. He caved.

Rowan crept down the stairs like he was carrying something fragile and radioactive at the same time. The portrait was clutched against his chest, back facing out, carefully wrapped in butcher paper and painter's tape like it might explode if handled wrong.

In the kitchen, the Aubreys were mid-laughter, cups of cider in hand, the tree casting golden light across the room. Selene turned first, her smile soft and quiet. Talia spotted the package immediately.

"Ooh, what's that?"

Rowan hesitated at the bottom step.

"It's—nothing. It's not ready. It's just... I mean, I was working on it, but it's not—"

"NOPE," Talia declared, practically skipping across the room to intercept him. "Unacceptable. You don't get to sneak around for two weeks and then not show us the thing."

He shrank back a little.

"It's just—"

She gasped. "Is it a drawing?! You brought us ART?!"

Rowan's ears went red.

"Talia—"

"I love it already," she beamed, hands on her hips. "I don't even care what it is. If it's a stick figure, I'm putting it in a frame and hanging it in the dining room like it's a Van Gogh."

Lyra leaned against the doorframe behind her, smug and unbothered. "He caved. I told you he'd cave."

Elysse looked up from her tea, eyes narrowing slightly in interest. "Let him speak."

Talia stepped back—barely—grinning like this was Christmas morning and her birthday had collided. Rowan looked at Selene. She just nodded once, calm and patient.

So, with a breath so small it barely counted, he turned the portrait around. And the room fell silent. Talia's eyes widened first. Her mouth opened slightly, then closed again like words had tried to form and gotten stuck halfway.

"That's..." she whispered, stepping closer. "That's us."

Elysse rose from her chair with deliberate calm, setting her cup down without looking. She crossed to Rowan slowly, studying the pastel lines and shapes with the kind of focus she usually reserved for historical documents or complex spells.

But Selene—

Selene didn't speak. Her fingers flexed once against the side of her mug, then stilled. She just stared at herself, at them, rendered with such care it was almost painful. The wicker chair. The softness in Elysse's gaze. The fire in Talia's laugh. The way Lyra somehow looked wild and composed all at once. And Rowan. In the middle of it all. Like he belonged there. Like he knew he belonged there.

157

It wasn't just beautiful—it was true.

Rowan's voice broke the silence, barely above a whisper. "I thought... if we ever had a family portrait, it should look like this."

Selene looked up at him. Her throat moved like she wanted to speak, but nothing came out.

Talia sniffled loudly. "Okay, rude. You could've just given us socks."

Lyra still hadn't moved. "This is the sappiest thing I've ever seen," she muttered. Her voice cracked halfway through it.

Elysse turned to Rowan and placed a hand on his shoulder. "This," she said simply, "belongs in the living room."

Rowan had just started to fidget under the weight of their silence-turned-affection when Talia suddenly clapped her hands.

"Okay!" she said, voice bright and watery. "Our turn!"

Rowan blinked. "Wait—what?"

"Oh, you thought we weren't going to give you anything?" Lyra said, her voice suddenly recovered, smug as ever. "That's adorable."

Elysse gave him a small, sideways smile. "Stay here."

Talia and Lyra practically vanished up the stairs, and for a moment the kitchen was full of confused tension and sniffling and someone muttering something about "dust in the air."

Rowan looked to Selene. She just smiled at him—warm, quiet, and whole.

Then the door from the front hallway creaked open, and Talia's voice rang out like a kid trying to keep a secret she was terrible at keeping.

"Close your eyes!"

Rowan did not close his eyes. He stood in stunned silence as Talia and Lyra wheeled it in. The chrome gleamed under the kitchen lights.

It was a bike. A blue bike. Sleek, new, and absolutely his. There was a small metal bell on one handle, a little headlamp wired to the front bar, and a woven basket—sturdy, perfectly balanced—attached to the handlebars.

"Tell me that basket's not for me," Lyra muttered.

"It's for groceries," Talia said quickly.

"Uh-huh."

Rowan just stared. He reached out, fingertips brushing cool metal, and felt the solid realness of it push into his chest like breath.

"It's... mine?"

158

"Of course it's yours," Selene said gently. "You've earned a way to get around without freezing your ears off."

Elysse folded her arms. "We also got you gloves."

"They're enchanted," Talia added. "Heat-retaining, wind-resistant, waterproof—"

"He's going to cry," Lyra stage-whispered.

"I'm not—" Rowan started, but his voice cracked and betrayed him. The bell gave a soft ding as he touched the handle.

Chapter Thirty-Eight — Christmas Morning

Talia burst into Rowan's room like a sugar-powered hurricane just after dawn. "MERRY CHRISTMAS!" she shouted, arms flung wide like she was announcing the Second Coming. "GET UP, IT'S PRESENT TIME!"

Rowan groaned and flopped onto his side, burying his face into the pillow. "It's not even light out."

"Christmas doesn't need sunlight!" she declared. "It runs on coffee and pure adrenaline!"

She had, in fact, already made a full pot of coffee. She had also, in fact, already drank half of it. Her foot bounced like it was trying to Morse code a sugar emergency.

Rowan peeked up at her, one eye squinting. "Are you vibrating?"

"I'm thrumming with joy. Now move!"

Down the hall, muffled groans echoed from other rooms.

"I hate this holiday," Lyra muttered from behind a closed door.

"You said that about Halloween," Talia called back.

"And I meant it both times."

Elysse appeared a moment later in a long sweater and socks, holding her own coffee like it was the only thing keeping her soul tethered to her body.

"Why," she asked dryly, "do we still let her have caffeine before 8 a.m.?"

Selene was already downstairs in the kitchen, calm as ever, humming softly as she reheated cider and laid out slices of leftover spiced bread on a tray.

Talia barreled past everyone and slid into the living room like a child on Christmas morning. Because she was, fundamentally, exactly that.

"Come onnnnnnn!" she whined from the couch. "If I have to wait another minute to watch people cry over homemade gifts and bad wrapping jobs, I'm going to spontaneously combust!"

Rowan stumbled down the stairs last, hair a mess, sweatshirt crooked, one sock missing. The scent of pine and cinnamon smacked him like a festive brick. Light sparkled off ornaments and someone's socks were already blindingly red.

"Is she always like this?"

Selene handed him a warm mug without answering.

The living room sparkled—lights glowing, gifts stacked, candles flickering in windows. Somehow, it felt cozy and magical and alive all at once.

For a second, he stood still... so this is Christmas.

The wrapping paper carnage had been cleared, the mugs refilled, and the Christmas music mercifully turned down. The kitchen table was a battlefield of leftovers: thick slabs of cinnamon bread, sweet potato hash, cranberry sauce that absolutely no one had asked for but still showed up, and a glazed ham that looked like it had been blessed by five generations of kitchen witches.

Rowan sat at the end of the table with a plate full of chaos and a second helping of spiced cider. Steam curled from mugs like lazy ghosts. Someone hummed along to the music—off-key, content. The glow from the kitchen windows made everything look a little bit golden. He didn't even ask what some of the things were. He just ate. It was all good.

"Did you try the stuffing waffles?" Talia asked, gesturing at something square, crispy, and vaguely savory.

"I have no idea what that is," Rowan replied through a mouthful, "but I would die for it."

Selene smiled softly as she passed him another slice of bread without a word.

They sat there a while like that—chewing, sipping, occasionally groaning with full-bellied satisfaction. It was quiet. Peaceful. Safe. And then Rowan cleared his throat, twirling his cider mug between both hands.

"Um... would it be okay if I ran to the Apothecary for a minute?"

All heads turned toward him.

"On Christmas?" Lyra asked, raising an eyebrow.

"I just... I need sealant. For the portrait. Before anyone touches it too much."

Selene didn't hesitate. "Yes, but you'll take Lyra with you."

Rowan blinked. "Why—"

"Because she's faster than calling an ambulance."

"I'm flattered," Lyra said, already reaching for her coat. "Also, I want a cinnamon roll."

"You've had three," Elysse pointed out.

"Yes," Lyra said, "and I want a fourth."

Rowan stood, grabbing his own coat. "I'll be quick."

Selene looked at him for a long moment. Not suspicious. Not stern. Just... quietly proud. "Be safe," she said.

He nodded. And just like that, Christmas morning shifted—from warmth and waffles to wheels on frosted pavement, with a portrait in need of protection and a witch in his corner. The town was still. Too still. Like a snow globe right after someone stopped shaking it.

The bike ride was chaos. Glorious, frosted, post-holiday chaos. Rowan had barely gotten two blocks before realizing the streets were half-iced and not even remotely salted. He pedaled slowly, trying to keep control, while Lyra—curled up smugly in the front basket in full cat form—looked like she was being chauffeured through a royal procession. Her green eyes scanned the street like a disapproving queen.

"You're heavy," Rowan muttered, trying not to skid as they rounded a corner.

"You're dramatic," Lyra replied. "Also, you're steering like a baby deer on roller skates."

"You could walk." His fingers were clenched so tight on the handlebars, he could feel the cold bite through his gloves.

"I could," she said, stretching luxuriously in the basket. "But then you wouldn't look like a fairy tale peasant delivering his witch aunt to market."

He huffed and kept pedaling.

When they reached the Apothecary, Rowan hopped off and leaned the bike gently against the back wall. Lyra leapt from the basket in one smooth, practiced motion, tail flicking as she landed beside the back door.

"I'll wait here," she said, curling up against the wall. "It smells like cloves and dignity."

Rowan rolled his eyes. "You mean like me?"

"You wish."

He smirked as he unlocked the back door and stepped inside. The shop was still and dim, full of the lingering scent of cedarwood, peppermint, and lemon balm. He didn't bother turning on the lights. He knew where everything was. His fingers traced over drawers and shelves until they landed on a small glass jar near the back workbench—label half-smudged, but unmistakable.

Sealant.

"Got it," he called. "See? In and out. Just like I said."

No answer.

The quiet felt too thick.

He paused, jar in hand. "Lyra?"

Still nothing.

He walked back toward the door. Opened it. Looked left. Then right. The basket sat empty. The snow beside it undisturbed. And suddenly, the cold air didn't feel so crisp—it felt wrong. Rowan's breath hitched, forming a cloud that vanished too fast. His fingers went clammy around the glass jar.

"...Lyra?"

Chapter Thirty-Nine — The Monologue

Rowan stepped into the cold, heart pounding like a drum behind his ribs. The sealant jar was still in his hand, but he'd forgotten it was there.

"Lyra?"

No answer. The air felt wrong. Heavy. Still. He turned toward the street, eyes scanning for movement—any movement—and that's when he saw her.

At the edge of the alley, half-covered in snow, lay a small black shape. Fur dusted in frost. Still. Unmoving.

Rowan's feet froze to the ground. It couldn't be—

That wasn't—

She couldn't—

"Lyra?" he whispered again, softer, like saying her name might wake her up. She didn't move.

His vision blurred for a second. His chest felt too tight, like it couldn't hold everything crashing inside him.

And then a voice behind him. Calm. Crisp. Distant.

"You're stronger than I expected."

Rowan turned. Lucian stood at the end of the alley. Perfect posture. Immaculate coat. Not a snowflake out of place, as if the storm knew better. He looked like he'd been waiting. Watching. Waiting for the exact moment Rowan would break.

Rowan's voice came out raw. "You did this."

Lucian didn't answer. Didn't deny it. His footsteps didn't crunch. Just the whisper of expensive soles brushing snow. He just looked at Rowan with cool, patient eyes.

Lucian stepped closer, slow and deliberate, like he had all the time in the world. His boots didn't even crunch in the snow. Rowan stood his ground—but only barely. His fists were clenched at his sides. His heart felt like it was trying to punch its way out of his chest.

Lucian stopped a few feet away and looked him over with a strange mix of curiosity and contempt, like he couldn't decide if he was looking at a puzzle or a disappointment.

"You've made quite the name for yourself," Lucian said at last. "The town's Christmas orphan. The sweet little boy who draws pictures and makes tourists feel better about themselves."
Rowan didn't answer.

Lucian tilted his head. "They talk about you like you're some kind of miracle. A redemption arc with mittens." He gave a humorless smile. "Do you really think that's your destiny?"
Rowan didn't answer. His throat felt lined with glass.

Lucian took one more step. "You could have anything, Rowan. Do you understand that? Power. Legacy. A world that listens when you speak. Not just a bike with a basket and a room in the attic."
Still, Rowan stayed silent. Not because he didn't have anything to say. Because if he opened his mouth, he wasn't sure what would come out.
Lucian's voice lowered. "Tell me, Rowan—do you really believe this town deserves you more than the world does?"
Lucian circled a few slow steps around him now, like he was admiring a painting only he could see.
"I knew it the moment I saw you," he said softly. "Something rare. Something born to shape the world, not be shaped by it. And yet... here you are. Drawing tourists and making soap."
Rowan didn't move.
Lucian stepped closer, close enough that Rowan could see the way his breath didn't fog in the cold.
"You think they love you. Maybe they do. But they don't understand you. Not the real you. Not the one that lives beneath all that control. You'll see it, eventually. You'll break something. Scare someone. They'll try to forgive you, but it won't be the same."
Behind Rowan's ribs, something began to crackle. Tiny sparks in the cold.
Lucian tilted his head. "They'll fear you, Rowan. And then they'll leave."
He was smiling now, soft and satisfied.
"It's not your fault. Power demands something more. Something bigger. You weren't made to be small." He leaned in. "You were made to be mine."
Rowan's voice came out level. Too level. Like something spoken through locked teeth and held breath.
"I'm going to tear your head off."

Lucian stood there, smug and untouchable, as if the world already belonged to him and he was just waiting for everyone else to catch up. Rowan didn't move. Didn't breathe. He was ice wrapped around fire, held together by the thinnest thread. Lucian leaned in slightly, voice silk-smooth and cruel in its gentleness.

"Is that any way to speak to your father?"

The air shimmered—just once. Like something was cracking beneath the skin of the world.

Rowan moved.

Chapter Forty — The Fight

Rowan slugged him.

Lucian's head snapped sideways with a meaty thud—

And then they were gone.

The alley blurred. Snow tore into the air. Metal groaned.

Rowan moved like a lightning bolt with bones. Fast. Angry. Reckless. He launched himself into the fight with zero hesitation and even less concern for how badly it might end. Every strike came like it hurt to throw but hurt more to hold back.

Lucian didn't meet him—he contained him.

Strike. Twist. Crack.

A rib bent. A shoulder wrenched. Rowan barely registered it.

He slipped from one hit into the next like he didn't care if it broke him.

Celerity blurred the fight into flashes—Rowan slamming Lucian against the brick wall. Lucian answered with a blow that threw Rowan clean across the alley. Rowan landed hard, bouncing, teeth bloodied, surging back up before he'd even stopped sliding.

Flesh split.

Breath tore.

Everything hurt.

None of it mattered.

Lucian was stronger. Trained. Precise.

But Rowan was willing.

And that was the most dangerous thing in the world.

A blur.

A slam.

A rib cracked on impact and Rowan gasped—but didn't fall.

He rolled, came up swinging, a sharp arc of movement that missed Lucian's throat by inches. Another flash—Lucian behind him, hand outstretched—

Contact.

Fingers clamped around the back of Rowan's neck.

Everything stopped.

Just for a second.

Biokinesis. The shutdown. Rowan felt it—the cold crawl under his skin, like invisible hands trying to take control of his body.

But nothing happened.

Lucian's grip tightened.

Still nothing.

Rowan's head snapped up, eyes bright with fury—

No.

Not bright.

Glowing.

Blue-white light surged behind his eyes. His skin flickered. Lucian's hand recoiled, fingers smoking. The glow wasn't light—it was heat. Radiating from his skin like it wanted out.

Rowan's breath hitched once.

Then he roared.

Lightning exploded from his body, a pulse of raw magic that lit up the alley like a bomb. Lucian was thrown back, coat scorched, boots skidding through the slush.

And Rowan didn't stop.

Lucian recovered fast.

Too fast.

He surged forward in a blur, ready to strike—

But Rowan was already moving.

A flash of movement. A dodge. A flicker of lightning behind him as he ran.

Lucian followed.

Strike—miss.

Lunge—counter.

Rowan hit and vanished again, slipping through the alley like smoke, vaulting over crates, crashing through the side gate of a snow-covered loading yard.

Lucian chased him, narrowing the gap with every step.

The fight became a rhythm—punch, flash, vanish. A heartbeat between each hit. Rowan's shirt was torn, his hands bleeding, boots sliding over ice—but he never stopped moving.

Lucian's face darkened.

He wasn't winning anymore.

He was chasing.

Another blow. Another dodge. Another blur—

And then Rowan skidded around the final corner. The hum hit first—low, dangerous. The smell of ozone curled through the air like warning.

Lucian followed—

And stopped.

Too late.

The ground beneath them was humming. The air buzzed.

They were surrounded by chain-link fencing. Massive transformers loomed overhead, static dancing across the coils. The substation was silent.
Waiting.
Rowan stood across from him, breathing hard, sparking with light. And smiling. The whole place felt like a breath held too long.
Rowan launched forward.
No hesitation.
No warning.
He tackled Lucian full-force, driving him backward in a burst of speed and fury. Sparks trailed behind them like comet tails.
Lucian slammed into the side of the transformer—hard.
Metal groaned. The ground vibrated.
Rowan pressed against Lucian's chest, locking him there.
The humming intensified.
And then—Rowan let go.
Not of Lucian—
Of everything else.
The lightning didn't strike.
It poured.
From the lines.
From the coils.
From the entire town.
  Electricity surged through Rowan, crackling up his arms, bursting from his chest, and into Lucian like he was nothing more than a copper wire. The light was blinding—brighter than day, hotter than fire, endless.
Lucian screamed.
Not in fear.
In indignation.
Rowan roared back, his voice lost in the chaos, throat raw, heart on fire.
Snow melted.
Metal sparked.
It was over; the storm faded.
Electricity hissed through the air, skipping across the metal in angry sparks before dying out.
Rowan staggered back.
Lucian slumped to the ground, body smoking, motionless.
He didn't move.
Didn't breathe.

Didn't look human anymore.
Steam curled off his coat. His face was... wrong. Stretched.
Flickering between human and something else.
Rowan stared.
His hands trembled—burned raw, still glowing faintly.
Lucian wasn't just defeated.
He was gone.
Rowan's breath caught. His vision tunneled.
He'd done it.
He'd killed him.
And if he could kill Lucian—
A man tied to him by blood, by power, by things too complicated to name—
Then who else?
What if one day it wasn't Lucian?
What if it was—
He turned.
And ran.

Chapter Forty-One — The Search

The lights in the manor suddenly went out and the warmth of the house was swept out at an unnatural pace; something was wrong.

Selene stood. "Coats."

Talia scrambled for her jacket. "What? Why—"

"Now."

Selene grabbed the keys, already moving. Elysse didn't ask—she followed.

Talia caught up, confusion mixing with fear. "Selene—what is this? Why—"

"Rowan."

Talia's questions stopped cold.

Selene opened the door and stepped out; the girls piled in behind her as tires crunched on fresh snow towards the apothecary.

The Apothecary was dark.

No lights. No glow from the windows. Just the sharp, metallic scent of something burned.

Selene pulled the car into the alley behind the shop.

Headlights swept over the snow—and stopped.

Talia gasped.

A small black shape lay motionless near the bike rack.

Talia was out of the car before it stopped. Her boots crunched through the snow, and she dropped to her knees as her fingers brushed the remains of a too familiar black cat laying cold in the now. She reached down carefully and scooped up Lyra's limp body and held it reverently against her coat.

Elysse turned away.

Selene gripped the wheel tighter, eyes narrowing. She looked past them, toward the distant column of smoke curling into the sky— too far for a chimney. Too wild.

She shifted the car into gear.

"Get in," she said.

Talia climbed in last, holding Lyra's body gently in her lap.

No one spoke.

The engine rumbled.

And Selene drove toward the smoke.

The substation was a war zone.

Chain-link fencing torn open. Snow melted to slush. A scorched transformer groaned, still sparking.

The air smelled of ozone.

An ambulance had arrived. Red lights pulsed faintly across the wreckage, casting long shadows over the snow.

Selene stepped out of the car.

Her boots hit the pavement with no sound.

She walked through the wreckage like she belonged there.

Two paramedics crouched over a blackened figure on the ground. Barely breathing.

Lucian.

His clothes were ruined, skin blistered, hair singed—but his eyes fluttered open when she approached. The sense of smug pride behind them was palpable even through the scorched eyelids. He didn't speak.

Selene turned toward the paramedics.

One opened his mouth to object—then stopped.

Selene didn't raise her voice. Didn't threaten.

She just looked.

"Release him to me."

The paramedic hesitated, then nodded.

Selene crouched, placed two fingers against Lucian's temple, and whispered something too quiet to hear.

She stood.

"Let's go," she said.

No one spoke. No one even breathed too loudly. They just moved, each step sharp with the kind of precision born from fear and inevitability.

Lucian sagged between them, heavy as stone, the stink of scorched flesh clinging to his ruined coat. When they laid him in the car, the sound he made was a wet, rattling thud that no one acknowledged. Selene drove. Her hands gripped the wheel like iron, the headlights tunneling through the black. The hum of the tires was their only heartbeat.

They carried ruin home—one wrapped in blood and ash, the other in silence and fur. And when Aubrey Manor rose from the dark like a waiting sentinel, it felt less like a return and more like a tomb opening to receive what was left of them.

Aubrey Manor was still dark. The power hadn't returned.

Selene lit the front hallway with a flick of her hand—just enough to guide them inside. No more.

Talia carried Lyra through the door, coat damp with melted snow. She moved to the living room, laying Lyra on the couch, smoothing her fur as if waiting for her to complain about the mess. Elysse and Selene didn't stop moving.

They cleared the dining table in seconds, pulling out herbs and poultices, anything they could use.

They hauled him onto the table, and the wood shuddered beneath his weight. He was breathing, but barely—each gasp shallow and broken, dragging through charred lungs. His skin was blistered and peeling, the smell of scorched fabric still clinging to him. Bones shifted wrong under his ruined frame. He didn't stir, didn't fight. Just lay there—burned, fractured, unconscious. Selene peeled the scorched fabric from his chest, ignoring the smell of burnt flesh. Elysse moved beside her, hands glowing with diagnostic light.

Talia stayed in the living room with Lyra, reverently. One hand resting lightly on her side.

And no one asked the question aloud; the silence asked it for them. Where was Rowan?

Chapter Forty-Two — The Return

Lucian's breathing had evened out.

Shallow. Ragged. But steady.

Selene stepped back from the table, hands slick with ash and blood. Elysse lowered her own, the soft blue light fading from her fingers.

"He'll live," Selene said.

Not triumphantly. Not even with relief.

Just fact.

She turned toward the living room.

"Has she come back yet?"

Talia looked up from the couch, blinking. "No. Not yet."

Selene frowned. "She's taking her time."

"She's dramatic," Elysse muttered, already washing her hands.

"She's dead," Talia said, dry as dust. "Let her have a minute."

Selene walked over, gazing down at Lyra's still form. Her fur looked cleaner now, brushed smooth, almost regal. If you didn't know better, you'd think she was sleeping.

"Come on," Selene murmured. "You made your point."

Nothing.

A beat of silence passed.

Then—

Lyra's tail twitched.

Talia stiffened; her gaze sharp.

"You witch—!"

Lyra's eyes cracked open.

She yawned, stretched, and without lifting her head, said, "Did we win?"

Lyra sat up fully now, ears twitching once before she yawned like waking from a nap instead of resurrection.

She blinked lazily at the room.

"Where's Rowan?"

Selene didn't answer right away.

Talia turned sharply, her brow furrowed.

"Selene?"

"He's not here," Selene said. "He wasn't at the substation. He's not at the Apothecary. I've scanned every ward, every path—he's not responding. He's gone."

The words hit the room like glass shattering.

Lyra's ears flattened against her head.

Then, in a blur of motion, she leapt from the couch—

And shifted mid-air.

Her boots hit the floor as a woman, tall, sharp-eyed, and pissed.

"I was dead for five minutes," Lyra snapped.

"You were supposed to be watching him," Talia said, her voice low and dangerous.

"I was."

"Not when it counted."

"Excuse me for dying!"

Talia took a step toward her, voice colder. "You think that's an excuse?"

"You think I wanted this?"

"You knew he was spiraling."

"I always know!" Lyra shouted. "But I can't follow him if I'm not breathing!"

"Enough," Selene said.

Both froze.

Her voice was quiet.

But absolute.

"We find him. Now."

The room buzzed with tension.

"What if we call the police?" Talia asked. "Say he's a minor—he went missing—someone will recognize him, right?"

"And then what?" Lyra snapped. "We explain how our magical foster child incinerated a man and fled the scene?"

Talia winced. "Okay, fair."

Selene opened her mouth to speak—

But Elysse was already moving.

She reached into the pocket of her cardigan and pulled out a tiny glass vial. A soft, silvery glow pulsed within it, swirling like smoke caught in moonlight.

"I made this," she said, holding it out to Selene. "It's keyed specifically to Rowan."

Selene took it instantly, fingers closing around it with rare, visible relief. "You used a resonance spell?"

"Hair from his brush," Elysse replied.

Talia blinked. "Wait. You stole his hair?"

"I borrowed it."

"Do you have one of these for me?"

"Yes."

"...Seriously?"

Elysse looked up, perfectly calm. "You live in this house. Of course I do."

Talia blinked again. "I don't know whether to be flattered or afraid."

Lyra shrugged. "Honestly? I feel safer."

Selene held the vial, the glow flickering and twisting like a compass, guiding her gaze toward the woods beyond Ashford Landing.

She closed her fist around it.

"Let's go."

Chapter Forty-Three — The Chase

The gas station buzzed with fluorescent hum and distant country radio.

Selene stood by the car, one hand on the fuel pump, eyes on the horizon. The lot was empty except for them and a flickering streetlamp that buzzed like it might short out at any second. A gum-stained bench sat under the grimy front window, abandoned coffee cup still steaming faintly beside it.

The cold wind tugged at her coat. It didn't seem to bother her.

The bell above the station door jingled.

Lyra emerged, arms overflowing with snacks—two oversized paper sacks crinkling in protest. Chips, chocolate, jerky, granola bars, energy drinks, gum, licorice, something blue that probably wasn't FDA-approved—

She shoved the bags into the backseat like it was standard procedure.

"You planning to feed a teenage boy or bribe one?" Selene asked, dry.

"Yes," Lyra said.

Selene replaced the nozzle, twisting the cap back on.

Lyra leaned against the car, eyes narrowing. "Was it really a good idea to leave Talia and Elysse with him?"

Selene's gaze didn't move. Only her jaw tightened.

"If he tries anything they'll kill him." she said quietly "and he knows it."

A pause.

"And he knows it." Lyra repeated softly without an ounce of her usual sarcasm.

The wind blew harder, tossing their hair and causing Selene's jacket to flap softly. Neither of them moved for a moment. Then slowly, Selene opened the door.

Back in the car, Selene sat behind the wheel and uncorked the charm.

The soft silver glow burst outward, then spun, orienting itself like a compass needle gone restless. It didn't point sharply—but it pulled, ever so slightly, like it wanted to move through her fingers and fly toward him.

Selene's gaze followed the line of motion—south, maybe southeast. Hard to tell exactly on back roads.

177

She frowned.

"He's moving," she said.

Lyra twisted around from the backseat, tearing open a bag of peanut butter pretzels. "So not passed out in a ditch. Great."

Selene didn't respond.

She tucked the charm into her palm. It pulsed once—cool as moonlight—before settling into a steady, urgent tug.

The tires crunched over frost-bitten pavement.

The charm tugged gently in her hand.

And somewhere ahead of them, Rowan kept walking.

They spotted him just past the treeline.

Selene brought the car to a sudden stop. The charm in her hand flared once, then faded.

There, curled against the base of an old pine, was Rowan.

At first, it didn't even look like a person—just a heap of soaked fabric tucked against the tree like windblown trash, knees drawn to his chest, arms wrapped tight, forehead pressed to his sleeves. His coat was soaked through. Fingers blue around the edges.

Snow clung to his hair. His lips were cracked. His breath came in short, shallow bursts that didn't seem to fill his lungs.

The car hadn't even stopped rocking before the passenger door flung open, wind rushing in like it wanted to steal the warmth with it.

She moved fast—but not loud. No shouting. No sudden movements.

She crouched beside him.

"Hey," she whispered.

Rowan didn't move.

His eyes fluttered open just slightly, unfocused.

"Lyra?"

"Yeah," she said softly.

A pause.

"...Am I dead?"

Her face twisted—but only for a moment.

"No," she said. "You're just cold, dumbass."

They had him bundled in the backseat, swaddled in borrowed jackets and half a blanket from the trunk. The car heater blew full blast, but Rowan still trembled.

Selene didn't say a word.

Lyra sat beside him, quiet, letting him come back to himself inch by inch.

And then—

"I planned it."

His voice was hoarse—strained.

Lyra looked over, her brow furrowing at the rawness in his tone.

Rowan didn't meet her eyes.

"I planned the whole thing. Weeks ago."

Silence.

"I knew he'd come after me eventually. I just didn't know when. Or where."

He coughed once, winced.

"So I started watching. Power lines. Grids. I memorized the layout of the town. I waited. I kept waiting."

His hands clenched in the fabric of the blanket.

"I knew I couldn't beat him straight. Not without something big. Something loud. But if I could get him to the substation…"

Lyra stared at him.

Selene's knuckles tightened on the wheel.

Rowan kept going.

"I just needed to make him chase me. That's all. One good mistake. One moment. That's all I needed."

His voice cracked. "I didn't want to kill him. I just… didn't see another way."

Selene finally spoke.

"There is nothing wrong," she said, "with defending yourself."

Rowan went quiet.

Selene didn't raise her voice. Didn't soften it, either.

"You survived a man who's taken down warlocks ten times your age. You outsmarted him. And you came home."

Rowan looked down at his hands again.

Then Lyra exhaled—long and dramatic.

"Oh, for the record?" she said, leaning back in her seat. "He's not dead."

Rowan froze.

"What?"

"Lucian. Not dead. Very crispy, extremely pissed, probably smells like overcooked bacon—but not dead."

Rowan blinked. "But he wasn't—he didn't—"

"I have excellent hearing, genius. I woke up on the couch and heard Elysse say he's stable. Breathing. Toasty. But alive."

Rowan slumped against the seat like someone pulled the plug on his spine.

Selene just kept driving.

Chapter Forty-Four — The Reckoning

The wind howled once through the porch rafters, then died.

The front door creaked open.

Rowan stepped inside, moving slowly, every muscle stiff from cold and strain.

The house was warm. Too warm. Someone had stoked the fireplace too high.

But the heat didn't matter.

Because Lucian was there.

Lucian sat upright on the couch, wrapped in bandages like a half-mummified king. Burn cream caught the firelight, and the rawness of his skin gave him the look of something only half-finished.

And watching.

His knees wanted to buckle. His chest felt too tight. But Rowan didn't flinch.

He just met Lucian's eyes and said, voice low and even:

"Next time... I won't hold back."

Lucian didn't respond.

Rowan turned and headed for the stairs.

Behind him, soft paws pattered across the floor.

Cat-Lyra followed close at his heels, tail swaying smugly like she'd been in charge of the whole thing.

Rowan didn't look back.

He didn't need to.

The next few days felt... wrong.

Not loud. Not hostile.

Just wrong.

Rowan kept mostly to his room. He said it was to recover, but no one believed that—not really. He needed space. Distance.

The door stayed shut more often than not. When it opened, it was only long enough to slip downstairs, grab food, and vanish again.

Lucian made himself scarce, too—though not entirely by choice.

He gravitated toward whatever space was the least occupied at any given time. The study. The sunroom. Sometimes the porch, bundled in a borrowed coat and blanket.

He never asked for help.

He never spoke.

And no one asked him to.

The house shifted around them—quietly avoiding the parts that creaked.

Conversations dropped when Lucian entered a room.

Footsteps slowed near Rowan's door.

Even Talia didn't shout.

The tension didn't explode.

It just lingered.

Like the weather before a storm.

Selene found him in the sunroom.

Lucian sat alone in the corner chair, swaddled in a too-large sweater that wasn't his. His bandages had been changed. His skin still looked like ruin beneath them.

He didn't glance up when she stepped in.

"Lucian," she said. "We need to talk."

A beat passed.

Then he looked at her.

Still proud. Still distant.

But weaker. And he knew it.

Selene didn't sit. She stood, calm and unwavering, the soft creak of the wood beneath her feet the only sound in the room.

"You have two choices."

Lucian's expression didn't change.

"You may stay," she said, "and work—truly work—to become the father Rowan deserves. To heal. To listen. To grow into someone worth knowing."

She let that settle.

"Or," she continued, "you may leave. And you may not return until Rowan is old enough to make that decision for himself."

Lucian didn't answer.

But he didn't need to.

The weight of it hung there—like the first breath after drowning.

Lucian smiled.

Not kindly. Not gratefully.

It was the quiet, infuriating smile of a man who believed he'd just won a game no one else agreed to play.

Lucian stood, slowly, his face still that mask of cold confidence.

But something in the way he spoke, the way his words hung in the air, made Selene's stomach twist.

"One day," he said softly, his voice almost a whisper, but carrying the weight of a dark promise, "Rowan will come looking for me."

His eyes met hers—calm, calculating, still convinced of his own superiority.

"And when he does, we'll fulfill what was always meant to be."

The words hung between them, thick and unyielding. Selene stood perfectly still, the faintest flicker of something—maybe uncertainty, maybe anger—passing across her face. But she didn't respond. Her silence was her response. It was enough. It had to be.

Lucian turned toward the door—

but paused.

Just for a breath.

His hand hovered over the handle, fingers twitching with the ghost of a thought he hadn't voiced until now.

"He never used a single defensive spell," he murmured. Not to Selene. Not to anyone. Just... aloud.

"You didn't train him to protect himself."

He looked back, grinning, eyes sharp with new understanding.

"You trained him to win", and then, with a slam of the kitchen door, he was gone.

Chapter Forty-Five — Worthy

The room was still—not silent. The radiator hummed low. Floorboards creaked in the walls, old wood shifting like it remembered something. But everything else had gone quiet, like the house itself was holding its breath.

Rowan lay on his bed, arms behind his head, staring at the ceiling as if it might give him the answers he was looking for. The silence felt heavier than it had before.

The door creaked open.

He didn't move.

Didn't need to.

Selene stepped inside. Her presence filled the room without needing words.

She didn't speak immediately.

Rowan's breath caught before he could say anything. His thoughts were tangled up—he didn't know how to explain the mess inside his chest. All he knew was that everything felt wrong, heavy, like something was pressing down on him from the inside out.

"...I'm sorry," Rowan said quietly, barely above a whisper. His voice cracked slightly, but he didn't look away from the ceiling. "I should've asked for help. I thought if I could just handle it myself, none of you would have to deal with it. But all I did was make things worse. I almost got someone killed. I almost..." He swallowed. "I almost..."

His voice trailed off, his chest tight. He didn't need to finish. He didn't want to.

Selene crossed the room, her steps soft but deliberate, and sat on the edge of the bed, near his knees. He still didn't look at her. She let the quiet stretch, just long enough for him to breathe through the words he couldn't say.

Then—"No," she said softly, her voice calm and sure, but with something unspoken beneath it. "This one's on me."

Rowan didn't speak right away. He let her words sink in. Slowly, he turned his head to meet her eyes. The weight in his chest hadn't lifted, but it was different now. Lighter, maybe, in a way that didn't seem to make sense.

Selene exhaled, slow and quiet. Almost a sigh. Almost a smile.

For just a second, her hand lingered on his shoulder.

When she drew her hand back, and the warmth of the moment stayed between them, unspoken, but felt all the same.

"Rowan," she said, breaking the quiet. "I raised Lucian differently."

"I told him his power was his purpose," Selene continued, her tone reflective. "That he was born to fix things. To save the world." She paused, her eyes distant, as though lost in a thought that didn't quite belong here. "But I never taught him to live. Not really. I thought I was doing the right thing, but I was wrong. I taught him how to measure himself by what he could change... but not how to be whole, how to live with what he couldn't fix."

She met his gaze again, softer now. "I don't want that for you."

Rowan didn't answer immediately. His mind spun in a thousand directions, but her words resonated deeply. Slowly, he sat up, his voice barely above a whisper.

"Maybe. But it was still my fault. I didn't ask. I didn't say anything. I just made this plan and waited for it to explode." He looked down at his hands, quiet for a moment. "I thought I could control it, but I ended up hurting everyone."

He looked back at her, eyes full of uncertainty. "What do you do," he asked, "when you make a mistake that big?" He picked at a frayed thread in the blanket beside him, like he could unravel the answer if he pulled hard enough.

Selene leaned forward slightly, brushing a bit of hair from his forehead, her touch warm and steady. "You make sure," she said, her voice unwavering, "that you become someone worthy of it."

Rowan sat quietly, absorbing her words. He nodded once, his chest feeling lighter than it had in days, though the weight of the past still lingered in his bones.

"Yes, ma'am," he said.

Selene's breath slowed, just the slightest exhale. Almost a sigh. Almost a smile.

And for just a second, her hand lingered on his shoulder. Not as a witch. Not as the matriarch of an ancient family.

Just as his mother.